Also by Cynthia A. Graham

Beneath Still Waters

BEHIND EVERY DOOR

a Hick Blackburn Mystery

by

CYNTHIA A. GRAHAM

Blank Slate Press | Saint Louis, MO

Blank Slate Press
Saint Louis, MO 63116

For information, contact
Blank Slate Press at 4168 Hartford Street, Saint Louis, MO 63116.
www.blankslatepress.com
Blank Slate Press is an imprint of Amphorae Publishing Group LLC
Manufactured in the United States of America
Cover Design by Kristina Blank Makansi
Cover Art: Shutterstock / IStock
Library of Congress Control Number: 2016931059
ISBN: 9781943075188

For my Uncle J. W. Howard,
and all those who came back forever changed.

BEHIND EVERY DOOR

I

"Slow down," Adam complained as the squad car bottomed out again sending shockwaves through his spine and splattering the windshield with mud.

Hunched over the steering wheel, Hick flipped on the windshield wipers and squinted into the distance. "I can't. This one is personal."

Sheriff Andrew Jackson "Hick" Blackburn and Deputy Adam Kinion, Hick's brother-in-law, were headed west along Number Nine Ditch. The vegetation on the left was soggy and sparse, the yellow grass bent and crippled by too much water. On the right, tiny cotton plants struggled to emerge from beneath a field of gritty mud and pools of standing water. The dirt road used by the Army Corps of Engineers was routinely maintained, but the late spring rains had given it a beating and the squad car jolted heavily, tires spinning in washed out ruts.

"There they are," Adam said, pointing at a teenager who waved at them from the top of the levee. Hick pulled in beside a rusted, ancient pickup, slammed the car in park, and jumped out.

At the top of the levee, the air was like a living thing, wrapping hot, suffocating arms around them, squeezing lungs and making it hard to breathe. Everything smelled of mud and standing water and blood and death. Below them stood another teen and nearby, half-submerged in the ditch was the body. One arm clung crazily to the lower limb of a young tree so that the head and right shoulder remained above the water line. A foot in either direction would have landed the corpse in the ditch where it would have likely been carried on to the river, never to be found.

"Hey Sheriff," Eben Delaney said, holding out his hand. Hick shook it and noted the scanty bucket of fish that would most likely be the Delaney's midday meal. Tenant farmers who lived in a tar-paper shack between Cherokee Crossing and Pocahontas, Arkansas, the boys had been the sole source of income for their family since their father had died in prison thirteen years earlier. At this time of year, before cotton chopping and picking began, Hick knew money was scarce.

The drainage ditch was nearly full, and Hick didn't have far to go to get to the body. His feet slid as he scrambled down the embankment, and the small hope he'd allowed to linger quickly vanished. Gladys Kestrel, the high school secretary, was dead. He didn't need Jake Prescott's assessment. The swollen, gaping wound on the side of her head covered in thick congealed blood and gnats testified to the cause of death. He removed his hat and ran his sleeve across his eyes, wiping away the stinging sweat. He gagged and covered his nose with his handkerchief as he surveyed the rise above her.

Adam moved a branch of the small tree and knelt beside Hick. He turned to Eben. "What happened, boys?"

Jed Delaney, Eben's younger brother, clambered through the muddy grass. "Don't you put this on us."

"Hush, Jed," Eben said, but Jed went on. "We didn't do no wrong, so don't you put this on us."

"Just tell us what happened," Hick ordered.

"Don't say nothin'," Jed warned.

"You crazy, you know that?" Eben told his brother. Turning to Hick he said, "Me and Jed come out afore sunrise to catch a mess of fish for the young'uns at home. We done been to number six ditch but they stopped biting so we come down here. We was walking the levee when we spied some dogs at something. We thought maybe it might be a deer and good eating so we run up to 'em and chased 'em off. That's when we found her. I seen her in town before and knowed who she was right off."

Involuntarily, Hick shuddered. He remembered Gladys at her desk outside his father's door at the school. More than the high school principal's secretary, she was Hick's advocate whenever he found himself in trouble. She never failed to give him an encouraging smile before he went into the office. He remembered her appearance, always neat, always fastidious and glanced down at the figure before him. "How long ago did you find her?" he asked Eben.

"Judging by the sun, I reckon about nine o'clock."

Glancing at his watch, Hick noted it was a little past ten.

The sound of a vehicle struggling through the slick, sandy mud caught his attention and he looked up to see Doc Prescott's car bumping along the rutted road.

"Then what did you do?" Hick continued, turning his attention back to Eben.

"Jed wanted to run off, but I knowed you to be a fair man and told him we didn't have nothing to fear. I left him here to keep the dogs away and drove off to the gas station and told 'em to call you. Then I come back here fast as I could."

"Did you touch anything?"

"No, Sheriff. Soon as we seen it was a woman we knowed better than to mess with her."

"When you were walking the ditch did you notice any cars or any people out here?"

"No," Eben answered. "There weren't a soul in sight."

Jake Prescott's car stopped beside the squad car and the doctor climbed out and paused, lighting a cigar and eyeing the levee disdainfully.

Hick made his way to where the doctor stood by his car. "We'll set up the tent and bring her over here if you like," he said.

Jake shook his head. "I want to see where she is and what she looks like." He chewed his cigar and looked at Hick. "It's definitely Gladys?"

"It's her."

"What would she be doing out here? It doesn't make any sense."

Hick helped the doctor climb the levee, in spite of the older man's assertion he needed no assistance. It was a small rise, not more than six feet, but the slippery, wet grass made climbing difficult. "Morning Eben, morning Jed," the doctor said by way of greeting and Hick suspected as an excuse to pause and catch his breath. "Your mama any better this morning?"

"She's in right good spirits today, sir," Eben replied. "Her rheumatiz is still painin' her, but her heart ain't thumpin' in her chest no more. We thank you for askin'."

"Good, good," Jake answered, pulling out a handkerchief and wiping his brow. "You tell her I'll be out in a day or two to visit."

"Yes, sir," Eben answered him. "I expect she'll look forward to it."

As Adam set to work putting up a tent down by where the cars were parked, Jake reluctantly accepted Hick's help and the two picked their way down the slippery slope to Gladys's body. The doctor knelt in the mud and brushed away the buzzing flies. He turned Gladys over and shook his head in dismay. The dogs had chewed off much of her lower lip, but the gash on the back of her head was the only mortal wound visible.

Hick pointed back at the levee. "I figure she rolled down the levee, there where the grass is smashed flat."

The doctor glanced up and then turned back to the body. "She was killed before last night's rain. Most of the blood's washed away, but there's enough left to attract the dogs."

"Water table's so high, there's no way to get tire prints. The road's a muddy mess," Hick added, silently cursing the sandy, delta dirt.

"But why in the hell would anyone kill Gladys?" Jake said, getting to his feet with a grunt. "She's the most harmless person in town." The moisture from the mud and grass had begun to seep between the seams of their shoes and the cold, gritty sand saturated their socks. Brushing away the loud flies, Jake said, "Let's get her out of here."

Eben helped Hick with the distasteful task of carrying the body over the top of the levee while Jake followed at a slower, more careful pace. The body was on the examining table by the time he reached the tent.

Hick winced at the damage done to Gladys's face by the dogs. She had always been a neat dresser; her plain, old-fashioned clothes suited her. He had known her his entire life and had never once seen her without lipstick or glasses. To see her like this seemed an outrage.

Jake palpated her head and parted her matted hair to get a better look, "Her skull's not fractured." Taking his cigar he pointed to her right temple. "There's bruising here. The blow was hard enough to cause her brain to slam up against the other side of her head. She died instantly."

"But not hard enough to crack her skull?" Adam asked from the doorway. "What about that bruise on her cheek? Was there a struggle?"

"There's no visible evidence of a struggle," Jake replied. "This bruise is lividity. The blood pooled there after she snagged on the tree."

"It seems like if she'd put up a fight there'd be some evidence," Hick said. "Her clothes aren't torn, no other visible blows …"

Jake took a drag on his cigar and let the smoke curl out of the corner of his mouth. "I'll check under her nails at autopsy but you're right, there are no visible defensive wounds. No bruising on her arms or hands. No injuries but her head and what the damned dogs did."

Adam's eyes scanned the expansive, isolated cotton field surrounding them. "How the hell did she get out here?"

Hick shrugged. "She was either dumped here or killed here. If she was killed here, she had to have trusted her killer or been coerced."

"Coerced?" asked Jake.

"Generally, you'll go with someone if they've got a gun to your head," Hick answered.

"But why kill a poor, defenseless, school secretary?" Adam said. "And look at her, still fully clothed. She's not rich, so it couldn't have been about money. The usual scenarios don't seem to fit."

Hick looked into Gladys's face. In the moments before her death, did she know what was about to happen? Who would hurt such a harmless person? Who brought her to this place? He searched her eyes for answers but they were dilated and sightless. Sighing, he closed them forever. She would take the hard-won knowledge with her.

"Beg pardon, Sheriff," Eben's voice called.

Hick walked out into the sunshine and spied a dark sedan heading toward them. Calling back to Adam, he said, "Murphy's here. Try to keep him ignorant for as long as possible."

Adam exited the tent and walked alongside the levee to intercept the troublesome newspaper reporter.

Jake joined Hick in the sunshine and shook his head. "Wayne Murphy is a pain in the ass. How's he here so soon?"

"If Eben went to Wally's station to use the phone, you can bet Wally didn't waste no time tellin' everyone he ran into that a body'd been found. In fact, I wouldn't be surprised if Murphy pays some of these folks for tips."

Eben cleared his throat. "Do you reckon Jed and me can go on? Mama worries when we don't get home time for dinner."

"You can go," Hick told him. "If I have any more questions, I know where to find you." Pausing he added, "Don't say anything to Wayne Murphy about what you found."

"Yes, sir," Eben answered. Jed gave Hick one last distrustful glance as the two young men climbed into their truck. The starter rattled hesitantly and the engine fired, mis-fired, and then back-fired finally sputtering to life. The truck clattered away and Hick watched them pass Wayne Murphy's sedan without a pause.

"I'll finish the autopsy in the office," Jake told Hick as they reentered the tent. "I'll do my damndest to find anything to help you find her killer, but I'm pretty sure we've found the cause of death."

A flood of memories washed over Hick as Jake covered Gladys's face with the sheet. Gladys at her desk every morning before any student or teacher set foot in the school house. Gladys locking the door of the school behind them as Hick and his father made their way down the front steps on cool autumn evenings. She had been the secretary at Cherokee Crossing High School for thirty years, longer than Hick had been alive. She was kind, benevolent, and trusted by every person in town. To Hick she was family. He looked Jake in the eye, his rage demonstrated in his cool, calculated speech. "We are going to get this son of a bitch," he said slowly. "By god, we're going to get him."

2

Gladys Kestrel had lived most of her adult life in an old boarding house owned by Miss Audie Briggs. It had once been a stately home with a wide brick porch and one dormer window that jutted out proudly above it. Years earlier, when Miss Audie had several renters, the place had bustled with activity. Now, the only renter was Gladys, and the house showed its age with rotting window frames, gutters filled with sprouting maples, and mole tracks crisscrossing the yard. Two overgrown trees hugged the front, covering the windows and shielding its inhabitants from the outside world. The whole place seemed trapped in the past, as if every creak and sigh was a reminiscence.

Hick knocked on the screen door and Miss Audie shuffled to answer. She was a large woman in a worn house dress. Her breasts hung pendulously to the sides and her back was bent forward. "Oh, mercy," she said, smoothing back her gray hair and opening the door. "I just got off the phone with Deputy Wash. I don't know where Gladys is, but she ain't been home since yesterday. I'm out of my mind with worry."

Hick and Adam entered the room. The corner table was piled with newspapers. A plate of barely touched biscuits and a half-empty cup of coffee sat on a small tray. Miss Audie's breakfast. It had hardly been touched.

"Miss Briggs," Adam said touching her shoulder. "We got some news for you. Why don't you have a seat?"

Miss Audie's face whitened. She grasped Adam's hand. "I had a feeling. There's been an accident. Is she okay?"

"Why don't we sit down, Miss Audie," Adam said leading her to the plump chair in which Miss Audie spent most of her days. He sank into the worn sofa across from her and spoke gently. "Ma'am, Gladys is dead."

Miss Audie stared, first at Adam and then up at Hick as if hoping he would contradict the report. Then her face crumbled. Plump jowls began to wobble, her forehead wrinkled, and her lips quivered. She let out a wail that took hold of Hick's spine and twisted. The wordless grief erupted from somewhere deep inside the old woman, and the two watched helplessly as a landslide of sorrow nearly buried her. She pulled a handkerchief from a pocket in her house dress and covered her face, howling in agony.

After a few moments, Hick reached out and touched her arm. "Miss Audie, can I get you something? A glass of water?"

She shook her head and wiped her nose, Finally, between sobs, she croaked, "How? How did it happen?"

Hick hesitated, glanced at Adam, and finally said, "Ma'am, we think Gladys was murdered."

Miss Audie's eyes widened and her mouth gaped open. "What? But why?"

"That's what we aim to find out," Hick said. "Do you know if Gladys had any enemies or anyone who might have held a grudge against her?"

"She didn't have an enemy on this whole green earth. Why every child that went through that high school looked to her as a friend. They were always coming over to visit, to just sit and chat."

"Has anyone in particular been coming over and spending an unusual amount of time with her?" Adam asked.

"No," Miss Audie said. "She ain't had as many visitors since the school closed." She paused. "In fact, she's been a little down-hearted lately."

Hick sighed. The Cherokee Crossing High School where his father had once been principal had closed the previous year. Dwindling enrollment was the latest indicator that the town, a once vibrant farming community, was facing a slow demise. Gladys, like so many others, had become a relic, once revered and treasured and then tossed aside and forgotten.

"When you say down-hearted, what do you mean?" Hick said.

Miss Audie hesitated. "I never pry into the affairs of my renters. I don't snoop and don't like those who do. I didn't ask no questions, and Gladys was always so private about her personal life. But I did notice that she seemed preoccupied lately. Like something was preying on her mind and she was tryin' to puzzle it out."

"And you don't have any idea what or who might have been on her mind?" Adam asked.

Miss Audie knitted her brow at him. "Like I said, I don't pry."

"But you and Gladys were friends," Hick prodded.

"It ain't possible to not be friends and love a person who lived in your home with you for thirty years. Every day Gladys got up and went to the school. She went to church on Sundays. She always paid her rent on time. She might have never had a suitor and no family ever visited her, but she did have friends. Yes, of course, I was her friend." Miss Audie's eyes filled with tears again and her lips trembled. "I don't understand. Who would want to hurt someone like that?"

"When did you see her last?" Hick asked.

"Why yesterday morning we ate breakfast together right here in this room, same as every day. We had our coffee and she read the paper."

"Did you see her leave the house?"

"No. But she always went for a walk in the morning before she went to the school building. She left every day at the same time, about 6:30 in the morning. When she didn't come back after her walk I just reckoned she went straight to school, she's been known to do that." She paused. "She can't seem to stop going to that place. I don't think there's any real work left for her to do, but every day, same as clockwork, she gets up, eats breakfast, and goes there. I says to her, 'Miss Gladys, what can you possibly find to do at that school? It's been closed up for a year. Why don't you just stay home one day?' But it was like she just couldn't stay home, like she had to go there."

"And when she didn't come home last night?"

Miss Audie shrugged. "I didn't think much of it. At first. I reckoned your mama come by and asked her to dinner. People was always trying to pull Gladys out of that school building and back into the world." She sniffed loudly. "I just went on up to bed at about eight o'clock. To be truthful I was a little put out that she didn't come home for dinner 'cause we had talked about what we was having just that morning." She sniffled and her mouth turned down into a pained line. "I never dreamed anything might've happened to her. I didn't even know she wasn't here until the morning." A tear spilled into her lap and she dabbed at her eyes with her hankie.

Adam leaned forward. "Can you think of any reason why Gladys would be up at the drainage ditch?"

"The drainage ditch?" she asked, her voice a low whisper as if she didn't want anyone else to hear. "Which one?"

"Number nine," Adam said.

"Nine?" Audie repeated. "How on earth would she get there? Why, it's a good five miles from here."

"You don't remember seeing or hearing a car?" Hick asked.

"No, and Gladys couldn't abide by 'em. She don't like automobiles one bit. I can't believe she would get into somebody's car."

"Well, she got out there somehow," Adam said, "and I'm pretty sure she didn't walk."

"Gladys in a car …" she muttered to herself in disbelief.

"Can we see her room?" Hick asked.

With a deep sigh, Miss Audie pushed herself up from her chair and looked around expectantly, as if Gladys might come down the hall any moment with a fresh cup of coffee. Then another sob broke free and she shook herself and said, "I'll take you."

The three climbed the dusty stairs to a small landing where a table festooned with several dead and dying house-plants sat in front of the dormer. Hick and Adam exchanged glances. Clearly Miss Audie's housekeeping had suffered of late. The old woman hesitated in front of the door to the left of the front window. "I never go in here," she said. "I always prided myself that my renters had their privacy." She opened the door to the small space Gladys had called her own. It was a decent sized room that contained a single bed, dresser, chifferobe, desk and chair, and it was neat and tidy, a stark contrast to the shabbiness outside the door.

"Thank you," Adam said. "If we need anything, we'll call."

Miss Audie nodded and went back downstairs, her tread slow and heavy on each step.

The two men took in the room. "What are we even look-ing for?" Adam asked.

"I'm hoping we'll know when we find it." Hick picked up Gladys's purse from the bed. "Look at this." He peered into the purse, dumped the contents on the bed, and then opened the wallet. "Funny she didn't take this with her. Looks like everything is still here."

"What the hell would Gladys have to steal anyway? We all know she didn't work at the school for the money."

Gladys's room reminded Hick of her office. Meticulous. Nothing out of place. "No sign of a struggle." Hick walked to the window and pulled aside the curtain. In spite of the tree branches that shrouded the house, he could see the driveway and had a clear view of the street in front of the house.

Adam opened the desk, an antique drop-front secretary with a variety of small drawers and cubby holes. He opened a cigar box and shuffled through a stack of papers. "These all appear to be letters from students." He shook his head. "Damn shame. Everyone loved her."

"Not everyone," Hick corrected. He opened the chifferobe that contained Gladys's clothes, clothes that were tailored, and, Hick supposed, elegant in a way, but that had remained unchanged since the days of Hick's youth. At the bottom were several neat stacks of Cherokee Crossing High School yearbooks. The school had been Gladys's family, the only one she could claim. "We'll have to go through 'em. Maybe there's something in there."

Hick then opened the top drawer of Gladys's dresser and timidly pawed through the delicates. They were all folded one like the other, placed neatly in the drawer. There were no messages from scorned lovers, no angry letters. The room was like Gladys herself, unassuming and ordinary. It was not the kind of place tragedy visited and Hick got the feeling that the room itself was perplexed as to why two men were in there poking around. As they continued looking, the phone rang downstairs and they heard Miss Audie's voice rise and fall with a whimper

Hick was searching another dresser drawer when a tap sounded at the door. It creaked open and Miss Audie peered inside. "Sheriff, that was Doc Prescott. He asked if you could stop by the undertakers and take some clothes for Gladys's buryin' tomorrow." She began to sniff and looked into Hick's face. "Do you think I oughta go on down there ... just to see her?"

Hick crossed the room and patted Miss Audie's shoulder. "No, Miss Audie. Ain't no call for you to go down there and see her. I wish I could un-see her."

Miss Audie stared as realization swept over her. "Poor Gladys," she moaned.

"Can you pick something ... that would be appropriate?" Hick asked.

"Doc says it won't matter much. The coffin lid's gonna have to stay closed." Miss Audie shook her head and said with resolution, "Still, Gladys would want to be decent." She moved toward the chifferobe and opened the door. "I reckon this is the nicest thing she has," she said pulling out a simple black dress that Hick had seen Gladys wear many times. "She's worn it to functions for years." Glancing at her own abundant figure she added, "She hardly seemed to change."

Hick knew what Miss Audie meant. When Gladys arrived in town she couldn't have been much more than twenty years old. When Hick was a child and first became aware of Gladys, she was barely thirty and yet she seemed ancient as if life had already wearied her. It wasn't as much that she hadn't aged as that she had simply always been old.

"I think that will be perfect," Adam said taking the dress from Audie who scrunched her face so as not to tear up again.

Audie stared at the dress in Adam's hand. "I never thought I'd bury Gladys. I always expected I'd go first." She pulled out her handkerchief. "But I don't reckon there's any way of really knowing who's gonna do the buryin'."

"No, ma'am," Hick agreed. "I don't guess there is."

∾

After leaving the dress with the undertaker, Hick made a detour to Doc Prescott's place where he found Jake sitting on his front porch swing. Like usual, the aroma of Doc's cigar greeted Hick as he climbed the steps.

"Did you find anything?" Doc put a foot down and stopped the porch swing. Hick lit a cigarette and took a seat beside the older man. He took a long drag and exhaled a great cloud of smoke as Doc pushed off and set the swing going again.

"Her room was spotless. We still have more to go through, but Miss Audie seemed taxed, and we needed to get the dress over to McDaniel's for the funeral. We'll finish tomorrow. What about you? Did you find anything?"

"No broken fingernails, no scratches, no defensive wounds. I can tell you there was no struggle at all."

"Strange," Hick said, deep in thought.

Jake inhaled and then reached over the porch rail to tap ash into the bushes, "By the way, how's Maggie?"

Hick laughed. "Tired as hell. Jimmy keeps her up all night, and she's so afraid he'll wake me that she just walks the floors with him. I told her to get some rest, but … well, you know Mag."

They both looked toward the horizon as thunder rumbled and the sky darkened in the distance. A breeze picked up and rustled through the trees, but still the smoke hung in the air as if unwilling to move on.

"Yes, I know Maggie," Jake said with a smile. "And you know her nature. She'll work herself to death if you don't watch it. You have to help her as much as you can. Her delivery was rough … it'll take her some time to recover."

"I know, I—"

"Hick, don't let this town and this job take you away from what's important. I know how you felt about Gladys. We all loved her. I know you have to find out who did this, and I don't doubt you will. But be careful."

Hick turned toward Doc. "What do you mean be careful?"

Jake exhaled a smoke ring and watched it dance and twirl before him in the soupy air. "You have a way of takin' everything to heart … you always have. When you have a puzzle in front of you, it's like you can't see anything else. You almost killed yourself two summers ago workin' on the Thompson case." The doctor watched as the storm clouds rose and billowed. Finally, he took another drag, the red end of the cigar glowing in the ever approaching darkness. "Just remember, there was a sheriff in Cherokee Crossing long before you were born, and there will be a sheriff after you're gone. Maggie needs you now. Don't lose sight of what's important."

A cool gust of wind was followed by thunder rolling long and heavy across the flat delta plain. Large drops of rain began to polka-dot the sandy driveway. "I best get home before this picks up," Hick said rising from the swing. "It looks like it's gonna be another gully washer." He looked at Jake and saw the concern in his old friend's eyes. "I understand what you're sayin', Doc, I really do. But I gotta find this guy."

"I know," Jake answered. "And you will. Gladys may not have had family, per se, and she didn't deserve to be dumped out by a ditch. I know you'll find out what happened, and you need to. But I worry. That's my job. You know I told your daddy I'd watch over you, and I plan to keep doing just that. I want you to promise to take care that you don't let this one eat you alive the way the last one did."

Hick flicked his cigarette into the yard. "I won't, Doc. At least I'll try not to."

Jake sighed and stood up. "That's all I can ask."

3

As so often happens after a storm, the next morning dawned bright. The small scudding clouds that remained scurried briskly across the sky and birds sang happily from their perches. The pressing humidity had evaporated overnight leaving air that was freshened and cool in its place. Smells of lilac, rain, and coffee greeted Hick as he stepped into the kitchen where Maggie sat at the table feeding the baby from a bottle.

"Are you sure you want to go?" Hick asked, reaching into the cabinet and pulling down a coffee cup. Even with her olive skin he could see dark circles ringed her eyes.

"Hickory, you couldn't keep me away from this funeral," she said with a note of surprise. "Why would you ask such a thing?"

"I heard you walking the baby last night, and I know you didn't get much sleep." He poured a cup of coffee and leaned against the counter. In reality, he had been awake, staring at the ceiling when Jimmy had begun to whimper.

Maggie had crept from bed, and he'd watched her shadowy form pick up the baby. He told himself it was the heat that made sleep difficult, pretending the images of Gladys's face and the smell of death weren't there with him in the room, causing his heart to pound painfully and sweat to soak the sheet beneath him.

"I haven't slept much in months," she reminded him. "That's nothing new, and it would be disrespectful not to go. I loved Gladys." She sat the bottle on the kitchen table and put the baby on his stomach across her knee gently patting his back. After a quick burp she picked him back up and cradled him. She ran a finger across Jimmy's plump cheek and looked up at Hick. "I think he's starting to look like you."

To Hick he looked like every other baby, but he wasn't about to say that to Maggie. Instead, he crossed the room and put his hand on her shoulder and peered down into the boy's face. Hick loved his son, but he could never shake the feeling that the child was an intruder. Diapers hung in the yard and the never-ending chores of washing clothes, boiling bottles, and mixing formula exhausted Maggie. Hick's schedule was so erratic that lately the two of them seemed to move in different worlds.

"How 'bout I bring you home after the service and you skip going to the cemetery?" Hick offered, taking a sip of coffee. "The ground is wet and it'll save your nylons from all the burrs. You could come home and take a nap."

Maggie considered. "It is awful damp out there for the baby."

She would never stay home for her own sake, but Hick quickly took up the idea that the damp would be bad for the baby. "Jimmy's just now putting on weight. We shouldn't take any chances."

Maggie's pregnancy had been difficult. So difficult that she'd gone home to her mother's for four months before the delivery. By the time Hick had been allowed to see his wife, everything was neat and wrapped up and she presented the baby to him like some sort of Christmas gift ... a tiny bundle wrapped in blue. But her smile couldn't hide the pallor of her skin. There had been blood, lots of blood. And Jimmy had been small and sickly. After five months he was only now beginning to put on weight, and instead of making life easier, his appetite had grown more voracious and his demands more insistent. There was no rest in sight for Maggie.

She seemed to consider his words and he added, "If you would do this for me, I could get Pam to take Mom home. Adam and I have some work to do anyway. What do you think?"

Hick knew she was thinking it over by the furrow between her eyebrows. Finally, she agreed, "You're right. The last thing we need is for Jimmy to take cold again. Doc says he's really starting to thrive."

"And you promise to take a nap?"

She laughed. "Yes, if it'll make you feel better."

"It will," He kissed the top of her head, swallowed the last of his coffee, and put the cup in the sink. "I'll wait outside," he said and went out to the porch, lit a cigarette, and pretended his hands weren't shaking. He closed his eyes, took a long draw from his cigarette, and exhaled a ragged breath. His thoughts were running wild and he smelled death even in the clear spring air. "Stop this," he muttered to himself. "Stop this right now."

Gladys Kestrel's funeral was a hurried affair because she had lain in the ditch for at least a day. With no family, the citizens of Cherokee Crossing banded together quickly and raised money for a coffin and cemetery plot. Ted Wheeler, Gladys's pastor, was to officiate at the service.

Hick paused in the doorway of the Methodist Church and scanned the waiting crowd. His mother and Miss Audie Briggs—the closest thing to family Gladys had known in Cherokee Crossing—were seated in the front row. Maggie and the baby were already with Adam and Pam in the second row. He drew in a breath, clenched and unclenched his fists, and started up the aisle. The eulogy was to be delivered by the last principal of Cherokee Crossing High School, the man who had taken Hick's father's place, and the pews were full of former students and teachers. Most of the students had moved on, leaving Cherokee Crossing behind them, and Hick shook his head at the thought that Gladys's funeral was an unfortunate reunion.

The Reverend Ted Wheeler rose to the podium and the sanctuary fell silent. Wheeler was an old-fashioned lawgiver, a man who spoke with the authority of having been to the mountaintop, of having looked evil in the eye and survived, and his flock hung on his every word. The folks in Cherokee Crossing held him in awe, and his congregation wondered how they had had the great luck to attract and then keep such a man. Tall with thin, dark hair, large glasses, and a grim visage, it was impossible to divorce his imposing presence from the great tragedy of his life, of having his only child, seventeen-year-old Susie Wheeler, murdered in the backwoods of Jenny Slough some fourteen years back. Abner Delaney, Eben and Jed's father, had been charged with the murder and duly executed. Back then, murder seemed a rare and curious thing in Cherokee Crossing. But not anymore.

The Reverend stood at the podium, his piercing eyes searching into the very soul of each individual present. The quiet made some in his audience squirm. Finally, he spoke. "In His word, the Lord proclaims, 'Whoso sheddeth man's blood, by man shall his blood be shed: for in the image of God made he man.' This town has experienced bloodshed, again. And this town must demand an accounting for that blood. Gladys Kestrel deserved to live to a ripe old age and to be loved and respected by all who knew her. She did not deserve to die, and she certainly did not deserve to have her body dumped at the levee to be torn and mauled by dogs." He paused and looked down at the closed casket to let that reality sink in.

"But this was not to be. There is an element in this town, an element that is not like us. They do not respect human life the way we do. They are animals. They live off the land, but they don't work it. They expect to be cared for and to do as they please. And when they don't get what they think they deserve, they take it! They take with violence like the animals they are, like the dogs that mauled Gladys, and they have no remorse for the pain and suffering they leave behind."

Hick shuffled in his seat. The reverend's words were not consoling. They did not comfort. They incited. He could hear whispers behind him and the room seemed to swell with a quiet clamor. "What is he doing?" Hick muttered.

The reverend paused again and looked intently at the congregation. "You remember my Susie," he continued in a broken voice. "You remember how one day her life was taken from me. How it was taken from her mother and her friends. You remember the man who took it and how God saw fit to deal with that man by having him die in prison. You remember and you demand that the same happens to those boys who took Gladys from us."

Hick's heart dropped. Was Reverend Wheeler making an accusation from the pulpit? Did he know something? He glanced at Adam whose usually relaxed face was taut and strained. Adam shook his head in disbelief. Evidently, the fact that the Delaney brothers had found the body had become public knowledge. Hick turned, and out of the corner of his eye, saw the delighted face of Wayne Murphy, testimony to his part in spreading that news.

The reverend stood silently for another moment and his eyes lighted on Hick. He said nothing, but his expression was accusatory, as if wondering why the Delaney brothers were not at that very moment rotting away behind bars. Then, he turned and walked, back ramrod straight and head held high, to his chair while the organist played and the church soloist began singing "Amazing Grace." After the soloist sat down and the congregation wiped their eyes and stifled their sobs, one of the English teachers recited the Lord's Prayer and the Home Economics teacher read the 23rd Psalm. Then everyone sang Gladys's favorite hymn, "Blessed Assurance." Finally, George Shelley, the last principal of Cherokee Crossing High School, approached the podium. He seemed ill at ease after the reverend's speech and paused to take a deep breath. In the pause it was impossible to not compare the two men. Whereas Wheeler was grim and dark, George Shelley was tall, with a handsome and open, youthful face.

Hick recalled when his father hired George Shelley. Only a boy, he still remembered Mr. Shelley bringing his young wife by the house. They were new to Cherokee Crossing, and Hick's mother invited them often for dinner. Hick remembered his dad and George sitting on the porch swing after dinner while George's wife, Elizabeth helped with the dishes. George was extremely clever and no one was surprised when he was transferred midyear to a larger school in Pocahontas. After cancer forced Hick's father to stop working, George Shelley had returned as principal and then had the unfortunate task of overseeing the school's closure and transfer of the remaining Cherokee Crossing students to the consolidated district in Pocahontas.

George cleared his throat and brought Hick's attention back to the present. "It is with great difficulty that I stand before you all today," he began with evident emotion. "If you would have told me last year while Gladys and I were closing the school that in another year we'd be burying her, I would not have believed you. Gladys was so full of life. When the school closed, she personally sent every student a note of encouragement, reminding them that Cherokee Crossing High School had given them an excellent education, and that they had nothing to fear in Pocahontas. She was correct. Our students excelled in Pocahontas last year, in large part due to the foundation and example set here in Cherokee Crossing."

"Gladys was a private person. She never said a lot about herself, but she didn't need to. You knew who she was by the life she led. She was one of those rare individuals that everyone, without exception, liked and admired. I remember when Elizabeth and I first moved to Cherokee Crossing. It was Gladys Kestrel who invited us to church, this church. She made sure we felt welcome here, and we did. It is with gratitude that I remember her kind attention and the way all of you took us in."

"When we were closing the school last spring, she insisted I leave all the tedious paperwork in her hands. Knowing that I had a new job in Tennessee, she sacrificed her free time to close the school so Elizabeth and I could put our new house in order."

"The last we heard from her was at Christmas. She sent us a beautiful card and a fruitcake, and, of course, knowing Gladys as we all do, she sent the girls candy. I had no idea it would be the last time we would hear from her." He paused and closed his eyes. He began again, but his voice broke. Finally, he continued, "I don't know why anyone would hurt

Gladys. She was thoughtful, caring, and kind. She would go out of her way to give anyone a hand and never once thought of herself. While we can't make sense of it, we need to move on with our lives and honor Gladys by living our lives the way she lived hers, by helping our fellow man, lending a hand to those in need, and listening to those who have nowhere else to turn. That is how I intend to honor the life of Gladys Kestrel, one of the finest people I ever knew."

Loud sobs erupted from the front of the church and Hick recognized Miss Audie's voice. His mother dabbed her eyes with her handkerchief, and Maggie dug in her purse for a handkerchief, finally settling for the corner of little Jimmy's blanket. George's eulogy had been a beautiful contrast to the Reverend Wheeler's harsh, embittered accusations, and Hick was thankful that the funeral ended on a warmer note, one more fitting for a woman like Gladys Kestrel.

The Wanderlust Cemetery sat on the outskirts of Cherokee Crossing in the middle of an enormous cotton field. The small, scrubby trees scattered between the tombstones were sparsely leafed after the unusually cold, wet spring, and to Hick it seemed ironic that Gladys would be buried there. Wanderlust was not something with which she was afflicted. His mother said that Gladys arrived in Cherokee Crossing, Arkansas in 1918, one year after Hick's father had begun his teaching career, and she'd been there ever since.

No one knew where Gladys came from, but the Postmaster whispered of an envelope sent from a Memphis adoption agency stamped with, "Photo. Do Not Bend." It became common knowledge that twenty-year-old Gladys Kestrel had a son out of wedlock and Cherokee Crossing was her haven. This information made a brief impression and then was forgotten by everyone but Gladys. The mouths of the gossips were closed, largely due to her impeccable life.

The service was already underway when Hick, after taking Maggie and Jimmy home, arrived at the gravesite. His mother and Miss Audie sat beneath a tent that flapped in the cool breeze as Ted Wheeler read from the Bible. Cardinals sang *pretty-pretty-pretty* from nearby branches and puffy white clouds billowed above the damp-smelling earth. The typical, beautiful June morning was natural and right; the grief and pain of burying Gladys was unnatural and definitely wrong. Standing apart from the cluster of mourners, Hick watched the sad spectacle and tried to make sense of it all.

"Morning Sheriff," a voice said, breaking into Hick's thoughts. He shook the hand offered by Matt Pringle and the two men stood watching as the coffin was lowered into the ground. In spite of Matt's short-lived engagement to Maggie, the men had remained on friendly terms, Matt letting his disappointment fall effortlessly from him, as he had every other disappointment. He married a girl from the next town over and they were expecting their first child. In spite of his penchant for self-centeredness, he was one of those people hard to dislike. He cleared his throat and said, in a lowered voice, "I don't mean to step on any toes, and I ain't one to tell you how to do your job ..."

Hick looked at him in surprise.

"It's just this," Matt continued. "Wheeler, he might be a preacher and all, but you need to know, he's got a real vindictive side to him. My brother Ronnie dated Susie when they were in high school and Wheeler was over-protective. And I don't mean like other daddies who protect their daughters. I mean he was relentless."

"What do you mean by relentless?" Hick asked.

"He hovered like a mosquito, like Susie was his property to give to whoever he saw fit. Every date they ever had was in that house and within earshot of Wheeler. He was possessive and mean and he never forgave Abner Delaney for killing his little girl. I don't doubt his hate reaches far enough that he'd like nothing more than to see Abner's boys tagged for this crime."

Hick recalled what he knew of Matt's older brother, Ronnie. Because he was only ten years old when Ronnie Pringle died, he never knew the older boy personally, but he knew a great deal about him. In his time, Ronnie Pringle had been the big man on campus at the Cherokee Crossing High School. He was wealthy and attractive and favored with those blessings life is generally all too stingy in bestowing. Like Susie Wheeler, he never realized any potential he might have had as soon after graduation he was kicked in the head by a mule. They say he died instantly.

Hick thought of his wife's short-lived engagement with Matt, a younger, but otherwise almost identical version of his brother. He never understood Maggie's obstinate refusal to stop loving him when Matt Pringle could have given her so much more.

Matt bent down and picked a couple of burrs from his pant cuff. He straightened back up and put his hands in his pockets. "I know Eben and Jed. They've worked for me for years, and I don't reckon I can see them killing Gladys. But Wheeler can and does and what he said today is just the start. I know how he operates. His God is a God of hate and vengeance. I just wanted you to know."

"I gathered he already had his mind made up."

"And before he's done, half of Cherokee Crossing will have their minds made up, too."

Hick sighed and shook his head. The scratch of a shovel and the thud of dirt hitting the coffin marred the beautiful spring day "A damned shame," Matt muttered, and then clapped Hick on the back and turned to go.

Hick couldn't get Matt's words out of his head as he drove his mother back to the church for the funeral luncheon. She sat beside him quietly, a small, lace handkerchief held to her nose. He reached across the seat and squeezed her hand and she smiled at him through her tears.

"Gladys was a good person," she said in a quiet voice. "I feel like I've lost part of my family."

"I know, Ma."

"What do you think your daddy will say?"

Hick glanced at his mother and decided he misheard her.

"You don't think those boys …" she said with a sniffle.

"I don't know," Hick answered. "I can't believe it, but I just don't know."

He pondered the idea of Jed and Eben killing Gladys, but couldn't fathom them being cunning enough to call the police to throw the investigation off their trail. They weren't dumb, but they weren't shrewd either. And what possible motive could they have for the killing? He was still thinking of the two boys when they arrived at the church. Walking inside, he saw a group in what appeared to be a heated debate.

"Poverty is not a crime," Elizabeth Shelley, George's wife, was saying as Hick joined the group.

The reverend looked at her benignly as if taking into account she was simply a hysterical female and not fully aware of what she was saying or with whom she was speaking. "Perhaps not," he answered in a condescending voice, "but when the character of a man is so skewed that he can no longer tell right from wrong, he must be removed from society, regardless of the cause."

"And you feel no share in the responsibility for this 'skewing'?" Mrs. Shelley persisted. Mrs. Shelley's appearance belied a more passionate nature. She was a small woman with a face more intelligent than beautiful. At this moment, her light eyes flashed at the pastor. There were few women in Cherokee Crossing who would dare confront Reverend Wheeler, let alone engage him in debate.

Wheeler's eyes narrowed. "I have no responsibility in what hoodlums do. They do not share our values. They take what they can with no respect for humanity. For those of us who value mankind as being created in the image of God, what share can we have in their wrongdoing?"

"But, aren't the poor also created in God's image?"

"The poor are poor because of the sins of the fathers, the laziness of the mothers, and the will of the almighty. Who are we to question the will of God?" He noticed Hick and, anxious to extricate himself from Mrs. Shelley, demanded, "And what of the Delaney boys? Have they been arrested?"

"No, Reverend Wheeler. On what charge?"

The reverend stared at him, his eyes cold as icicles. "Murder, of course. You can't possibly think anyone else killed Miss Kestrel."

"Until Adam and I complete our investigation, I am keeping an open mind."

The reverend's lips thinned and pressed together in a scowl. "You can't be serious. Those boys are the fruit of Abner Delaney. Murder runs in the blood."

"Even if that were true," Hick countered, "I can't arrest them for what their father did years ago."

Mrs. Shelley turned back toward Reverend Wheeler. "Thank goodness there is someone left in Cherokee Crossing with a little sense." Addressing Hick she said, "If you're anything like your daddy, you won't let prejudice cloud your better judgment."

Hick blushed and shuffled his feet. "I don't intend to let—"

Reverend Wheeler exhaled loudly. "Intend," he repeated in a mocking voice. "Your good intentions may let two killers walk free. Even now, they're probably on their way out of town."

"That truck of theirs wouldn't even get them to Pocahontas. Them boys ain't goin' anywhere."

The reverend inched closer to Hick. "Have you seen a fox caught in a trap? They will gnaw off their own feet to get away. Those boys will be out of the state tomorrow if you don't get out there and arrest them today."

Hick stood his ground. Noting Wayne Murphy hovering he said, "Jed and Eben Delaney are not suspects in this murder. They are material witnesses, but that is where their involvement appears to end. Unless I have some kind of substantial evidence, I cannot and will not bring them boys in."

The reverend's face reddened. "The next time you look for your 'material witnesses' they'll be gone. I know how these people operate. They'll be gone and Gladys's blood will accuse you from the grave."

"That's a chance I'm willing to take." Hick nodded at Mrs. Shelley, turned from the reverend, and joined his mother and sister at a table where a glass of sweet tea waited for him.

Adam arrived with a heaping plate of food and took a seat across from Hick. "What the hell was that all about?"

"Apparently Wheeler has some sort of God-given ability to see into the hearts and minds of men that we mortals lack."

"He's gonna be a problem." Adam picked up a piece of fried chicken and bit into it.

Hick's sister, Pam, leaned forward. "Sounded like Mrs. Shelley was really giving it to him."

"Well, I'm glad someone has the nerve," Adam said through a mouthful of chicken.

"Tennessee seems to be agreeing with the Shelleys," Pam continued.

"I believe they'll be very happy there." Hick's mom patted Pam's arm.

"I reckon a change now and then can be a welcome thing," Hick said absently, his attention focused on Wayne Murphy who stood apart from everyone else, coolly observing the room as was his custom. Murphy caught his eye and nodded. Hick turned away. He took a long drink of his tea and looked at his brother-in-law. "Adam, you gonna be ready to get back to work any time soon?"

Adam stuffed a spoonful of mashed potatoes in his mouth, grabbed a chicken breast from his plate, and stood up. "Let's go get this bastard."

4

Stopping the squad car in front of the Cherokee Crossing High School, Hick and Adam climbed out. They climbed the acorn stained steps toward the whitewashed glass door. For over three decades the building had housed kids in grades seven through twelve, and yet in a year's time nature had already begun to reclaim its space. The gutter above the doorway had torn away from the building and rain pouring down the façade caused green mold and white mildew to grow on the bricks. Kudzu crept up the mortar and was beginning to spread across the front of the building. The lawn was overgrown, and thick weeds sprouted through cracks in the sidewalk. Several small trees grew up against the foundation along with various unidentifiable bushes. The windows had been boarded up, but some on the second floor already had holes from squirrels and raccoons. Hick imagined how sad all of this must have made Gladys as she watched the school's slow descent into decay.

Inside, the place was shrouded in darkness and eerily

empty. The two men pulled out their flashlights, and Hick noted the darkened rectangle on the wall where the portrait of his father, now hanging in his mother's living room, had spent so many years. The formerly gleaming linoleum floors were now covered in dust, and the locked trophy case which had displayed the baseball trophies of their youth now stood open, its shelves bare. The school closing had been a hard blow for the town, in particular for Gladys Kestrel. While most of the staff was able to find work elsewhere, Gladys didn't seem to have the energy to look. It was as if she was part of the brick and mortar of the building. She never ceased to come to her office every day, supposedly to clear up files and paperwork. But everyone knew that Gladys's whole life was wrapped up in that building. She couldn't stay away.

A gloom settled around them as they made their way down the hallway toward the principal's office. Hick opened the door to the reception area and then stepped into Gladys's office. It smelled musty and close but was still relatively organized. They ran their flashlights along the length of the room noting that everything seemed to be in order. The filing cabinets were emptied, their contents boxed and stacked in neat rows along the wall. With a glance at the door to his father's office, Hick turned to Adam. "Nothing suspicious here. No signs of a struggle. Everything's just as she left it."

Adam picked up a file from one of the boxes and shined his flashlight on it. "Where were these going?"

"I reckon to the county courthouse. Archives, probably."

Adam thumbed through the box. "A lot of people went through this school. End of an era."

Hick moved to Gladys's desk and sat in the chair. He looked at the files sitting on top of it and then at the box beside the desk. "It looks like she was almost finished. These are from 1949. She's got files from 1915 through '49. The school had a pretty good run."

"You think there's anything in these worth killin' over?" Adam held up the file in his hand.

Hick shrugged. "They're just student records. Grades, absentees, any kind of health or disciplinary problems."

"But there'd be a folder in here for everyone in town."

"Reckon most everyone in Cherokee Crossing at least went through eighth grade even if they didn't finish."

Replacing the file, Adam crossed the room and opened the door to the principal's office. Hick felt his heart constrict. He could never go into the office without remembering his father's patient face as they discussed his latest report card. Hick didn't know who had it worse; his father, being a principal with a poor student for a son, or himself, a poor student with the principal for his father.

A board had been removed from one of the windows making the room lighter than Gladys's office. In front of it sat a small table with three potted plants. In addition to the table, the room still boasted a desk, chair, and credenza, although the walls were empty and the credenza bare.

"I wonder what used to be here." Adam said, indicating a dark circle of wood that stood out from the light coating of dust on top of the credenza.

"It could have been anything." Hick looked around the room. "Maybe she moved one of these plants closer to the window."

Adam opened and closed all the drawers. "Looks like George cleaned everything out before he moved on to Tennessee."

The atmosphere of the office was neat and tidy and had the feeling of a place held in awe. Despite the light sheen of dust, it was a stark contrast to the dilapidated state of the rest of the schoolhouse. The floor looked like it had been swept recently, and the remaining houseplants were watered and well cared for. On the principal's desk an old lamp, two nameplates, and a marble pen stand were carefully placed like holy vessels on an altar. It felt more like a chapel than an office, but if it had any secrets, it wasn't telling.

The two men left the room and Adam closed the door behind him. Hick moved back to the files Gladys had been working on. Absentmindedly he thumbed through them. "I was hoping something would jump out at me, that something would feel wrong."

"Yeah," Adam agreed, flipping through the files in a different box.

"There's not so much as a file out of place."

Adam stopped and looked up at Hick. "That being said, where is 1936?"

"What?"

"Gladys was meticulous about keeping things in order. The box for nineteen thirty-six is missing."

Hick scanned the room. "No. It's over here, on this stack."

"Okay, but why would that box be out of place?" Adam asked. "Everything else is lined up neat as a pin." He opened the lid and shone the light on the files. "It's chock full, though. Everything in alphabetical order." He put the lid back on and turned to Hick. "Doesn't look any different from the other boxes."

"Adam, what are we missing?" Hick sat back down in Gladys's chair and surveyed the room.

"Hell if I know," Adam admitted. "Let's think. What have we got so far?"

"Well, we know Gladys didn't walk to that levee on her own and she didn't drive. She was taken to the levee, dead or alive, but we've been to her room and there are no signs of a struggle there or in here. Doc says she didn't put up a fight."

Adam nodded. "None of the usual motives for a random killing seem to fit. She wasn't robbed, she wasn't violated, and she didn't fight back." He paused and raised his eyebrows. "If it wasn't random, what's the motive?" He nudged a box with the toe of his boot. "Revenge?"

"For what?"

"Look at these files. Gladys had a lot of information at her fingertips. You think she found something and was blackmailing someone?"

Hick shook his head. "You figure Gladys for a blackmailer?"

"No, but I wouldn't have figured Gladys for a murder victim, either. Miss Audie said she took a walk that morning and then didn't come home. That she sometimes went straight to school from her walk. Something happened, and

I'm inclined to believe it happened—or at least started—here. Miss Audie says she never went anywhere else."

Hick was quiet for a long moment. "I don't know. Blackmail is so out of character for Gladys."

"If she was blackmailing someone it would make sense to meet in secret," Adam continued. "The only reason to meet so far out of town is to not be seen."

"What on earth could Gladys have known that would make someone kill her?"

Adam swept his arm around the room to take in all the stacked boxes. "She knew something about almost every single person in this town. There has to be something here in these files."

"School records?" Hick said. "You think someone would kill over school records?"

"It's all we have to go on, Hick. If she didn't fight, and she was alive, then she willingly climbed into a car, never dreaming she wouldn't return. There has to be a reason. It had to be someone she knew."

They were silent a moment, both of them looking at the office that would remain empty forever. Finally Hick decided. "We'll bring this box along. Maybe it's out of place for a reason."

"Where to now?" Adam asked as they squinted against the sun and climbed down the stairs to the squad car.

Hick put the box in the trunk and slammed the lid. "She wrote everything down. Maybe there's a note, something about an appointment she had with someone the day she died. We need to take a closer look at her room."

∽

Barefooted and wearing a faded house dress, Miss Audie was in the yard pulling Maple saplings from her defeated flower bed when Adam and Hick arrived. Wiping her dirty hands on the front of her dress she met them in the driveway.

"Oh, I hope you come to tell me good news," she said with a plaintive warble in her voice.

"We've got no news yet," Hick said, "but we need to go through Gladys's room again … if you don't mind."

She turned toward the house. "You go right ahead. I don't know rightly know what to do with poor Gladys's things. She got nobody to send them to, not that there'd be much to send."

With Adam behind him, Hick climbed the stairs and paused in front of Gladys's door. "I don't know why this is bothering me so much. We've searched places before."

"This is work. Forget this stuff belongs to Gladys and just get to it." Adam opened the door and moved toward the desk. He pulled out a drawer, spilled the contents onto the bed, and began sorting through them.

Hick sat in front of the desk and peered into the cubby holes. He spied a couple of letters to an attorney in Memphis and opened the top one. Scanning it, he turned to Adam, "This is a letter to a lawyer in Memphis. It looks like she's been trying to find her son."

Adam glanced up. "Does it say why?"

Hick shook his head. "No. He just says the agency is uncooperative and he needs a little more information." He pulled a bank book from the next cubby hole and opened it to the last page of entries. He stared at it for a moment, flipped the pages backward and forward. "Adam, take a look at this. Last page." He tossed the book on the bed.

Adam opened it and blinked. "Who the hell is Millicent Harris?"

"I don't know, but Millicent apparently has a little money."

Adam whistled. "Fifteen thousand dollars. Why would Gladys have this?"

Hick opened a drawer and pulled out a few file folders until he found what he was looking for. He lay it open on the desk and started riffling through the thick stack of bank statements. "Adam, what if Gladys was Millicent Harris?"

"What?"

"These bank statements are all addressed to Millicent Harris at a post office box in Memphis, and they go all the way back to 1920—right when Gladys showed up in town. But why would she feel she had to assume a new name?"

"And where did she get fifteen thousand dollars?"

"And why did she leave the money just sitting there?" Hick studied the statements. "As far as I can tell, there's never been a withdrawal and looks like there's only been two deposits. The first was for $10,000 in 1919 and another $5,000 deposited six months ago."

Adam whistled softly. "Hate to say it, but blackmail is looking more probable."

Hick frowned. "She couldn't have blackmailed someone from the school in Cherokee Crossing. She would have to blackmail the whole town to get that much money."

"We'll need to subpoena the bank records from the Central Bank in Memphis," Adam said. "Maybe they can tell us where the money came from."

Hick nodded and continued searching the desk while Adam pulled a small trunk from beneath the bed and opened it. Inside was a scrapbook containing letters, newspaper clippings, and photographs. There were the school pictures taken each year of Hick and Pam, and one of Hick in his army uniform sent home just before leaving for Europe. Behind those were the school pictures of George Shelley's girls, Lucille and Edna May.

Gladys saved every Christmas card ever received from the Blackburn and Shelley families, and the old-fashioned faded corsages given to her on her birthday were pressed neatly between the scrapbook's yellowed pages. Hick remembered the first year his father handed Hick the clear box with the corsage and gently nudge him toward Gladys. Hick was seven years old and Gladys's eyes had filled with tears. "Why thank you, Andrew," she said with a look of grateful delight. It occurred to Hick that his father was thinking of the son Gladys never knew when he persuaded Hick to begin the birthday ritual. It remained intact until he left Cherokee Crossing for basic training.

Newspaper articles announcing Pam and Hick's marriages and the birth of their children were glued in place along with others that dated back decades. Stories of the First World War, the Great Depression, and World War Two were saved along with more local items like Hick's election as sheriff and numerous gatherings, town events, and obituaries.

"She really thought a lot of your family," Adam said softly, holding a picture of him and Pam smiling happily on their wedding day.

"Mom and Dad always treated her like she was one of us." Hick sighed and turned his attention back to the desk. He pulled open a small center drawer in the old drop down and extracted a group of newspaper articles held together with a large paper clip. "This seems odd," he said, drawing Adam's attention from the scrapbook. "This is the article announcing Susie Wheeler's murder, and there are stories of Abner's arrest, trial, and execution here, too." Hick turned the articles over and ran his fingers over the back side of the newsprint. "Feel this. The paper is stiff. Maybe they were glued in the scrap book and she took them out."

Adam crossed the room and took the papers, rubbing them between his fingers. "That is strange. Let's see if there're blank spaces in the scrap book." He sat down with the scrapbook and flipped through the pages until he found what he was looking for. "Here. They were pasted in here," he said holding up the empty pages where there had been something glued and then removed.

"Why the interest in Susie Wheeler and Abner Delaney?"

"Hell if I know," Adam said.

Hick scratched his head. "How long ago did Susie die?"

Adam held up one of the newspaper clippings. "Says here 1936."

"The same year as the box of school files we've got in the trunk." Hick shook his head. "I don't get it. What's the connection?"

"Maybe something in all this will give us an idea." He pointed to the contents of the trunk where stacks of school newspapers and letters and other memorabilia sat beneath the scrapbook.

Adam handed the clippings back to Hick who stared at the story of Abner Delaney's execution. "It doesn't make any sense."

"No," Adam said. "But it is a strange coincidence that Gladys's body was found by Abner's boys."

"Shit," Hick muttered. "If Wheeler finds out he'll have this whole town screaming for their blood."

"Maybe he's right after all. Maybe she found something and threatened to blackmail the Delaneys."

"Threatened them with what? Abner's dead and the Delaney's are poor as dirt. No, I don't buy it. Besides, why would they call us if they'd killed her?"

"I don't know, but we need to figure this out quick. Between Wheeler and Murphy, things could get ugly real quick."

Hick looked again at the newspaper. No details about the crime, no motive, no evidence. Just an arrest and an execution. "Were you around when Abner Delaney was arrested?"

"Pam and I were engaged and Michaels told me to sit it out." Adam shrugged. "I honestly never knew much about the case. I was ... distracted."

Hick couldn't help but smile. "I remember."

At thirty-six, Adam Kinion had been a confirmed bachelor in Cherokee Crossing. It wasn't that women weren't attracted to him, he just always said he'd never met the right one. And then, within a matter of months, eighteen-year-old Pamela Jo Blackburn had converted him from an independent bachelor to a love struck, domesticated husband. Hick was only ten years old at the time, but he had liked Adam from the start and had come to respect and rely on his brother-in-law in the years that followed.

Hick pushed back from the desk and stood. "Here's what we need to find out: first, why was Gladys studyin' on a fourteen year old murder? And second, how in the hell did she get fifteen thousand dollars in the bank?" He put the papers back in the desk drawer and turned to Adam. "Get a hold of the judge to file the subpoena for the bank records. In the meantime, I'm heading out to the Delaney place. I want to ask the boys a few more questions."

5

The Delaney house resembled a wood pile with a rusty red roof. The whole place was set up on cinder blocks from the days when the Little River flooded. The steps to the front porch were treacherous and busted and the porch itself was teetering precariously on one end. There was an old tub with a washboard sitting inside of it and nearby an icebox that couldn't afford ice and was used, instead, to store potatoes. The pickup truck the Delaney brothers drove stood in the yard, looking more like a pile of rust than a working vehicle. The front door was without a screen and stood open to let in daylight, air, and mosquitoes. Hornets buzzed from a nest underneath a dilapidated porch roof from which several cats peered down. The whole place smelled of decay.

"Miss Delaney?" Hick called into the dark house.

A young girl appeared in the doorway, barefoot with a faded print dress. Thirteen-year-old Mourning Delaney and her twin brother Job had been born the year their father was executed in the penitentiary. She had little hope for an easy life. She was poor, she was ignorant, and she worked hard all summer chopping cotton to help put food on the table. In spite of these hardships, there was a simple charm about her that was hard to resist.

"Howdy Sheriff," she said with a smile showing a wide gap between her front teeth. She tugged at a blonde braid while balancing on one foot and scratching a mosquito bite with the other.

"Hey Mourning," Hick answered. "Eben and Jed at home?"

"No, sir," she answered.

Mourning's twin, Job, seemed to materialize from somewhere within the dark shack. "Hey, Sheriff," he said. He lacked his sister's charm and there was surliness to his face that was not so much meanness as just habitual.

"You seen Eben or Jed?" Hick asked the boy.

"Yeah," he answered. "They come home a couple of hours ago and Ma got on 'em right smart. Said to get their things together 'cause Smitty was gettin' a truck up to go on to Illinois for the strawberry pickin'. It's been warm up that way and Smitty said the berries was ready."

Hick frowned. This was not an expected development.

"Sheriff?" a weak voice called from inside the darkened shack.

Mourning turned and seeing something said, "Come in. Ma wants to see you."

Hick entered the house. The furnishings were sparse but the cabin itself was clean and tidy. Mrs. Pearl Delaney sat in a rocker near the stove in which a fire was burning despite of the mild June weather. She had a blanket over her knees and two thin gnarled hands rested on it. She was not as old as she appeared but hard work and sorrow had taken their toll. "What's this about, Sheriff?" she asked. "Why you need my boys?"

"They found a body yesterday morning while they were fishing, and I need to ask them a few more questions," Hick replied.

Pearl stopped rocking and sat forward. "Sheriff, you know I got little trust in the law after the way they did my Abner. Them boys didn't do no wrong and they's gone now for a week or two."

Hick shuffled uncomfortably. "Ma'am, I might need to bring them back. This is important. The woman they found had been murdered."

Pearl's eyes widened. "Just like Abner," she said breathlessly. "My boys is gonna get blamed just like Abner." Her eyes stared in front of her as if they were seeing a catastrophe unfold. "God's judgment," she muttered to herself.

"Ma'am," Hick tried to reassure her, "we ain't planning on charging your boys with any wrongdoing. We just gotta ask them some questions since they found the body."

Pearl fixed her faded blue eyes on Hick. "My Abner was walkin' in the woods and come upon a body and the next thing I knowed he was electrocuted. Iffen you take my boys in, they don't stand a chance. They's poor and uneducated and their daddy was a con. Don't you see? It don't matter iffen they did it or not. The decks already stacked against 'em."

Hick understood Pearl Delaney's fear. Abner's guilt would bleed onto his sons. Justice often eluded the poor. In spite of this, Jed and Eben had to be brought in. Hick believed the boys were at the wrong place at the wrong time, but with Reverend Wheeler's vitriol filling the minds of the townsfolk, they needed to be questioned to put the gossips to rest.

Hick knelt before the old woman in the rocker. He placed his hand upon hers and looked deeply into her eyes. "Miss Delaney, I need to talk to your boys. I need them to tell me some things to help me catch someone who killed an innocent woman. You understand that, don't you?"

She stared ahead and refused to meet his glance. "Nobody cared when my innocent man was kilt in jail. Nobody questioned the fool lawyer who was so drunk he could hardly stand at the trial. Nobody questioned the girl's daddy or the girl's feller 'cause they all had money and standin'. Nobody's gonna care when my boys get dragged to trial for somethin' they didn't do and when they get kilt nobody's gonna care. Nobody … but me. And nobody cares about me."

Hick sighed. She was right and there was no way he could deny it. He rose. "I'll do my best by your boys," he promised. "I got cause to bring 'em in and I got to do it. But I'll do my best to be sure to bring 'em home if they're innocent."

Hick rose and turned to leave only to be met by the wide stare of Mourning and the scowl of Job. He walked outside, the bright sunshine stabbing his eyes as he made his way to the squad car.

"Sheriff," a voice called. Hick turned to see Mourning running toward him, her bare feet flying over the dust.

She approached with a handful of grimy envelopes. She held them up. "Here. Ma wants you to look at these."

"What are they?"

"They's letters and notes sent to us from the prison. Ma don't even know what they say 'cause we never had none could read 'em to us, and Ma was too ashamed to ast anybody. Says maybe you can look at 'em and tell us what they say."

Hick took the stack of envelopes and noticed the neat handwriting. "Who wrote these?"

"They's a man at the prison who tried to help Pa. He wrote us them letters."

"Who?"

"Mourning? Get in here!" called Job from the house.

"Don't know," she answered and added, with embarrassment, "I reckon he thought one of us could read or he wouldn't have bothered."

"Mourning!"

She glanced at the house and then turned back to Hick. "I sure enough would like to know what Pa said," she said with a wistful note in her voice. It might comfort Ma some, too." Then she quickly turned and ran back inside.

6

"There's nothing unusual in them going to pick strawberries this time of year," Adam said after Hick filled him in on the details of his conversation with Pearl and explained where the Delaney brothers were. "But damn, it sure looks bad right now. People are gonna jump to conclusions."

"People have already jumped to conclusions." Hick looked wearily at the pile of work on his desk. In spite of the fact that the clock on the wall said two, it seemed the day had been endlessly long and there was a daunting amount of work yet to do. Hick, Adam, and Wash stood in front of a large table and looked at the box of files from the school and the trunk from Gladys's room, along with the Doc's report and various other pieces of potential evidence that needed investigating. The amount of letters and paperwork that had to be reviewed reminded Hick of a tangled mess of fishing line. It was snarled and twisted and caught on something deep, but he felt that at the bottom of it all lurked something important that needed to be carefully unwound. "What did Gladys get herself into?" Hick shook his head. What was she doing in secret that could have incited someone to such violence?

Lighting a cigarette, he looked at Adam. "So what about the money? What did the judge say?"

"He says it'll take the Central Bank in Memphis a few days to track everything down after they get the subpoena. It's been there a long time and fifteen thousand dollars is a lot of money."

"Holy Christ!" Wash looked up, eyes wide. "I didn't think there were any secrets in this town." While Adam had been going through the letters Gladys had received from former students, Wash had had his nose buried in the student files. "Fifteen thousand ... my, my ..."

Hick looked at the grimy stack of envelopes that Mourning Delaney had handed him. Why had Abner's story interested Gladys enough to be removed from the scrapbook? There was no way in hell the Delaneys had given Gladys five thousand dollars. What possible connection could there be? Hick sat the cigarette in the plastic ashtray, rested his elbows on the desk, and opened the oldest letter in the stack. The paper was wrinkled and creased and he could almost physically feel the yearning of Pearl and Mourning Delaney as they held Abner's words but could never grasp their meaning.

Dear Ma,
    I am settled here at Pinewood and it is not as bad as we had feared.

"Pinewood not bad?" Hick repeated to himself. He knew better. Pinewood Prison Farm was notorious for allowing prisoner "trustees" to guard other prisoners. It was a place of torture and brutality.

> *This letter is being written by a Catholic preacher who works at the prison. He has been very kind to me. I hope you can find someone to read this to you so you will know I am thinking of you and the young'uns. I hope you are resting up so you will have an easy time when the baby comes. I hope to write again soon. As long as I know you and the baby are safe at home I can stand anything.*
> *Your husband,*
> *Abner*

Hick shook his head. Abner never knew his wife had been carrying twins. They were born shortly before his execution and he never received the information.

In the midst of the letters, Hick found one that caught his eye. It was a note written to Pearl Delaney from the "Catholic preacher" himself. It read:

> *Dear Mrs. Delaney,*
> *Please do not think me forward in writing to you without Abner's knowing. I am concerned because your husband has flatly refused to file an appeal of his conviction. Without one, I fear his execution will take place before all the facts of the case can be investigated thoroughly. After speaking with him and getting to know*

him here, I feel he has a very good chance of winning an appeal. It is clear there was gross misconduct, not only on the part of the investigation but also in his defense at the trial. For my part, I believe that Abner Delaney is an innocent man and, therefore, am writing to beg you to come to the prison to convince him to do this. His life is at stake. Without this attempt, his death is imminent.
    Yours truly,
    Reverend Jefferson D. Grant

Hick dropped the letter and stared, sickened by the idea that Pearl Delaney never knew she could have helped her husband save his life. But why wouldn't Abner attempt an appeal? Was he guilty, completely disillusioned with the judicial system, or was there something more? The words "gross misconduct" and "investigation" stared at him from the page, stark in their implications. What did Sheriff Michaels do that caused this man to allege "gross misconduct?" As he pondered this question, the door to the station opened and Wayne Murphy sauntered in.

"I see you boys are hard at work apprehending Gladys's killers," Murphy said with a smirk.

The remark was met with silence, but Murphy was undeterred. "I don't reckon it matters to ya'll whether them Delaneys kill a couple more good citizens. It looks like your reading is more important than actually getting up and catching them." He sat on the edge of Adam's desk and leaned over trying to see what Adam was reading. "I've been watching from across the street and you ain't moved in over an hour. Gladys has been dead two whole days and in that time not one of you has had the gumption to go out and bring those boys in. You hoping maybe if you wait long enough the town'll do your dirty work for you?"

Again, silence. "You know," Murphy said, crossing the room and standing in front of Hick's desk, "I really worry about those Delaney boys, I truly do. Reverend Wheeler told his deacons yesterday if ya'll didn't hurry and lock 'em up, the church might just need to form their own posse. He says he knows how it feels to have someone you love taken away by a Delaney, and he doesn't want to see anybody else hurt. And don't think the town don't know they's still out there. Mizz Scott says they tried to steal her chickens and I hear the Ewells seen 'em in their garden. They say they's been skulking down along the ditches, hiding out." Murphy smiled, showing his new gold tooth. "Maybe I oughta just print all this in the paper. You could read it there since readin' seems to be about all you're willin' to do."

His statements were again met with silence. Wash slapped a file folder down and picked up another one. He leaned back and propped his booted feet up on the desk, completely ignoring Murphy's presence.

Murphy frowned, but went on, "Yep, I understand the good Reverend is fixin' to have a church meetin' to discuss self-defense. He's been preaching about how we got to protect our families from the likes of them." He knitted his eyebrows together. "Hmmm. Ya'll are as silent as a tomb today. Maybe you done brought them boys in or maybe they's gone, just like Wheeler said they'd be." A light went on his eyes. "Hellfire, you done let them murderers fly the coop, didn't you?"

Murphy's words were irritating, like the constant drone of a mosquito in Hick's ear. He felt his forehead grow hot and anger blurred the paper before him. "Don't look up, don't look up" he kept repeating to himself. Wayne Murphy knew exactly how to get to him, but he could not let himself take the bait.

Adam rose from his desk and stretched, yawning loudly. "I could use a break. You want to head over to the diner for some coffee?"

Hick smiled to himself. Murphy could get under his skin, but Adam was seldom bothered by anything. He stacked the letters and opened the drawer of his desk, putting them away. Looking up he said, "Why if it isn't Wayne Murphy. Is there anything we can help you with?"

Wayne harrumphed with exasperation. "You can help me by running those little bastards in so I can talk to 'em. I got papers to sell and not a lot to put in 'em. I'll put your picture on the cover, and we can find out why they decided to go bad. What do you say?"

"I'm sorry," Hick said. "Who exactly are we talking about?"

Murphy's face flushed with frustration. "Dammit, why are you always giving me the cold shoulder? Don't you know I can help you?"

Hick stood. "When I need your help, that'll be the day I resign."

The newspaperman's face creased in a wide smile. His

new tooth gleamed. "I'll be here to write it up, Sheriff. I guarantee that's a story that will go above the fold." He started for the door. "You fellas have a nice break. Sit back and drink your coffee and take your time while the rest of the town frets and fumes."

The door closed behind him, and Hick exhaled loudly. "That son of a bitch drives me nuts."

Adam was unconcerned. "You can't let him get to you." He turned to Wash. "You comin'?"

Wash ran his hand over his head and looked at the box of student records. "I'm thinkin' about clockin' out early and going on home to the Missus." The older man's face was tired and had an unsettled look.

"You go on," Hick said. "This'll still be here tomorrow."

Wash nodded. "I was afraid of that," he said with a wry smile. "Them files don't make for easy reading."

Hick and Adam left Wash behind and crossed the street to the diner. They took their regular seats, noting the scowls on several of the customer's faces.

"Dammit," Adam muttered. "Between Murphy and Wheeler we're gonna have a riot on our hands."

Shirley Daniels, the new waitress, came by to fill their coffee cups. She paused at the booth and cleared her throat. Hesitantly, she said, "Sheriff, I don't mean to be a bother … it's just … well, I get off late from here some nights and I gotta walk on home myself. Last few nights I seen someone in the shadows, out in back of the lot. I'm just a wondering … I mean …" She sat the coffee pot down on the table and bent toward the men, lowering her voice. "I mean, do you think it safe for me to walk home nights … with them Delaney boys running loose?"

Hick sighed. What was the world coming to? "Shirley, it might not hurt to have your daddy come get you at night … just until we figure this whole thing out."

"You reckon you'll arrest 'em soon?" she asked.

"If it's the Delaney brothers you're worried about, yes, I think we'll be talkin' to 'em pretty quick. Even if I locked them up, I still think you ought to have your daddy walk you home. For now."

"You don't think they did it?"

Hick shook his head. "I don't know."

She smiled a small smile. "Thanks, Sheriff. I'll tell Daddy what you said."

Adam took a large gulp of coffee. "Lived in this town all my life and never seen it so on edge. We've never locked our doors or worried about anything here."

"Times are changin'," Hick shook his head and stared into his cup.

"Well, what do you aim we do about all this?" Adam asked.

"We're gonna have to call in an All Points Bulletin on the Delaney brothers, if for no other reason than to keep them safe. I really don't think they killed Gladys, and I don't think there's much else they can tell us, but I'm afraid if they come back to town on their own things'll get nasty."

Adam nodded. "I'd hate to see 'em stroll into town unawares. Wayne Murphy's gonna make sure people get whipped up into a frenzy. Give him something for page one."

"Above the fold," Hick added with a smile.

The door to the diner opened and several more people walked in, their faces unusually sober and cautious. Hick took a sip of coffee, still mulling over the phrase 'gross misconduct' from the Catholic preacher's letter, and shook his head. "What do you think about what Pearl told me ... about Wheeler and Ronnie Pringle never even being questioned. Does that seem right?"

"Not to my way of thinkin'," Adam agreed. "Unless you have a confession, you keep asking—"

"And they didn't," Hick interrupted.

Adam sat his coffee cup down on the table and looked at Hick. "You know how it is ... right or wrong, they would never have questioned the richest boy in town and a minister when there was Abner Delaney. It just wouldn't happen ... not fourteen years ago."

Hick's face colored and he shook his head. "Bastards."

"I know how you feel, but remember who you're talkin' about. You're talkin' about Sheriff Michaels and you're talkin' about Wash. They're good people, but they're also human beings with inborn prejudices. When they see poor folks like the Delaneys, they see problems. To them it was only a matter of time before Abner Delaney done something wrong because that's just what they expected from him."

"Well it's not fourteen years ago ... it's today. We can't question Ronnie, but we can sure as hell question Wheeler."

"What do you propose we question Wheeler about? We got nothing to ask."

Hick sighed. "I don't know, but something is just not

adding up here. I want you to keep going through Gladys's things. Either she was hiding something or she found something. Either way, there has to be some clue there. There's no way in hell Gladys would have driven off with a stranger. Something she was doing in the last days of her life led to her killing. I'm going to find that preacher Mourning told us about. He said there were problems with Abner's conviction, and he seemed to think Abner was innocent. If he's right, whoever killed Susie Wheeler has been walking around a free man for fourteen years while Abner is cold in the ground and his family even worse off than before. If Gladys figured that out, it'd explain a lot."

7

The Pinewood Prison Farm had a nasty reputation for corruption and brutality, and Hick was not surprised at the abrupt, uncooperative attitude of the clerk he reached on the phone. He had better luck at the Diocese of Little Rock and was able to find the whereabouts of the Catholic "preacher" who wrote Abner's letters for him. Learning he was only an hour away in the small town of Broken Creek, Arkansas, Hick decided to pay him a visit. After calling in the All Points Bulletin on the Delaney brothers, he drove home to tell Maggie it would be a late night.

"You're not going to the prison are you?" she asked from the doorway to their bedroom.

"No," Hick answered tossing his old shirt into the hamper and pulling on a fresh one. "The preacher is in Broken Creek. I don't have to drive all the way to Pinewood, and I'm glad. I don't want to be anywhere near that place."

A small furrow deepened between Maggie's eyes and Hick knew she wasn't satisfied. "Why do you have to go?"

Moving into the kitchen, he grabbed a thermos and filled it with coffee for the journey. "I don't know what I think I'll find, but none of this adds up. Why would the Delaney brothers kill Gladys, and what did Gladys have to do with any of this? This preacher thought Abner was innocent, and I want to know why. And if Abner was innocent, who the hell killed Susie Wheeler? I can't help but think there might be a connection." He glanced up. Maggie's mouth was turned down in a frown as she unconsciously swayed back and forth, holding Jimmy tight. She wasn't pouting, she wasn't the kind. But something had her bothered. Hick crossed the room to her and ran the back of his index finger along the baby's cheek. He held her gaze and saw concern. "What is it Mag?"

She hesitated. "Broken Creek. Ain't that where Earl Brewster is?"

"I won't be seeing Brewster." He stepped back to screw the lid on the thermos. "I don't want to see Brewster."

Earl Brewster, the sheriff of Broken Creek, Arkansas had been the key witness before the Federal Grand Jury in one of the first cases of Hick's law enforcement career. The older man had relished criticizing Hick's handling of the investigation. Brewster gloated after the case had been dismissed, but Hick felt his boasts were ill placed. No consideration was given to the fact that the dismissed perpetrators were Brewster's first cousins. The family was also connected to the Attorney General who was running for governor at the time. In spite of these irregularities, the failure to prosecute the Smith brothers had shaped Hick's first term as sheriff, largely due to the uncomplimentary and exaggerated reporting of Wayne Murphy. It remained a wound that wouldn't heal. One that, in fact, always seemed about to break open and bleed again.

Maggie brushed hair from her damp forehead. "I wish you didn't have to go anywhere near that man."

"The preacher works at a Negro church," Hick said. "Brewster wouldn't be seen on that side of town unless he was fixin' to arrest someone." He grabbed the thermos and forced a smile. "Don't worry. I've got no business with him."

Her eyes held his. They seemed to be questioning him, trying to figure out if he was okay. She sighed and glanced out the window. "You best be going. I think it's gonna rain."

There was a sadness mingled with resignation in her voice that caused Hick's heart to expand. He pulled her close and inhaled the scent of her hair. "I'll be back tonight. It ain't much more than an hour away."

"I'll keep your dinner warm."

Hick looked into her face and cupped her chin. "You're not afraid of being alone, are you?"

Maggie brushed that aside. "Of course not ... I'm—"

"Because if you are," Hick interrupted, "you could stay at your mother's, or my mother's."

"I'm not afraid," Maggie said with a note of finality in her voice. "And I won't be alone. Your mother and Mrs. Shelley are coming over to see the baby tonight. I'm not worried for me. It's everything about this. It's Gladys and Brewster and that prison. Promise me you won't go to that place. I've heard awful things about it."

Hick pushed a hair back from Maggie's face and looked into her eyes. "I promise I won't go to the prison. I've got no call to go there, and I agree with you. I wouldn't send my dog there. And if this Catholic preacher can tell me something, anything, to keep me from sending Eben and Jed there, it'll be worth the trip."

Maggie managed a weak smile. "You're right. If you can spare Miss Delaney that pain, then I suppose you need to go."

Hick kissed the baby's forehead. "I'll be back later."

She nodded.

He paused at the doorway. "I want you to keep this door locked."

"You can't be serious," Maggie said. "I've never locked a door in my life and it's so hot—"

"I know it's hot," Hick snapped with an irritated edge to his voice. He closed his eyes and sighed. "Someone killed Gladys Kestrel, and I have no idea who or why anyone on earth would do such a thing. Until I figure it out, I want you to keep the door locked all day, every day. Especially when I'm gone. Okay?"

She nodded. "I will, Hickory."

"Thank you." He started to pull the door closed behind him, but she caught it.

"You be careful. Promise me."

"I promise."

He paused at the car and pulled a Camel from the pack, tapping the cigarette on the back of his hand. He was unreasonably agitated as he forced a smile and waved at Maggie.

He climbed into the car and pushed in the lighter, then jumped at the sound of it popping out. He lit the cigarette and took a deep draw. The smoke in his lungs calmed his nerves. Then, he turned the key and waited until the door was firmly closed behind Maggie. Coaxing the car into reverse, he headed south.

A storm rolled in before Hick had been on the road a half hour. Big, loud drops slapped at his windshield and soon gave way to sheets of water cascading from the roof only to be interrupted by the wipers. Thunder rumbled and water pooled in low places on the road. The ditches were already full with days and days of rain and the muddy water sat, stagnant, swelling the mosquito population.

The rain had not let up by the time he arrived at Our Lady of Sorrows Church, on the outskirts of Broken Creek. It was a small building with a muddy parking lot and behind the church were train tracks and a large cotton gin. On the other side of the dirt road lay a cotton field that stretched out to a distant break of trees. He parked, put his jacket over his head, and ran through the rain to the church. Inside, he closed the door against the wind and shook his jacket out.

"Good afternoon, sir. May I help you?"

Hick turned to see a young black woman in a starched, white blouse eyeing his uniform with barely concealed suspicion. She clutched a shiny patent leather purse, evidently preparing to leave for the day.

Hick removed his hat. "Hello, ma'am. Is the preacher at home?"

She suppressed a small smile. "Father Grant is in his office." Glancing again at Hick's uniform she asked, "Do you have an appointment?"

"No, ma'am," Hick answered.

"I'll tell him you're here."

She left the room and Hick stood in the entryway. It was small and shabby but otherwise impeccably clean and organized. The walls were adorned with religious pictures, mainly cheap prints in cheaper frames. The patchwork rug was frayed at the ends and thin spots testified to years of wear. And the room smelled musty, like the roof might be leaking. After a moment, the secretary opened the door and beckoned Hick forward.

"Here's the lawman come to see you, Father," she said. As Hick entered, she smiled, nodded, and left the room.

Father Jefferson Davis Grant, sat in a worn leather desk chair, and regarded Hick a moment. The expression on his face wasn't unfriendly, but there was a reserve, a resignation, and a bitterness that Hick could not account for.

"Won't you have a seat," he said in a deep, resonant voice.

Hick sat down and glanced around the room. On a credenza behind the priest sat a covered typewriter and on top of the cover rested a mound of paper. Above all this hung a cross-stitched sampler that read, *What is man that Thou art mindful of him.* To the right of the typewriter sat a bottle of brandy and a half-empty glass. There were files everywhere, their contents spilling out every which way and Hick was amused to note that this room was as disordered as the other was neat.

Hick expected a bookish, small man, but Father Grant was neither. He was tall with a heavy brow, thick beard, and an expression hovering somewhere between distrust and disillusion.

"What can I do for you?" he asked in a tired voice.

Hick hesitated and then answered, feeling foolish. "I don't rightly know if there's anything you can do for me."

The priest looked surprised. "Care to explain?" he said with a slight softening of attitude.

"You were chaplain at the Pinewood Prison Farm about fourteen years back, right?"

Grant's mouth smirked with disgust, as if he had eaten something sour. "I was."

"And I reckon the prisoners came to you with their problems … or confessions."

"Some did."

Hick leaned forward. "I don't exactly know how to put this so I'm just going to say it. About thirteen years ago a man named Abner Delaney was executed at the prison for the murder of a young woman in Cherokee Crossing. Two days ago his boys came across the body of a murdered woman in a drainage ditch and called police. I don't know how, but the murder of this woman may be connected with the murder of the girl Abner Delaney was executed for killing."

The priest reached toward the credenza and drained the glass sitting on it. "And what has any of this to do with me?"

Hick felt himself growing frustrated because he couldn't think of anything. He knew he was grasping at straws, but straws were all he had. He shook his head. "I don't know. I really don't know. Abner's daughter handed me a stack of letters sent to her mother from the prison. They were written by you."

Father Grant turned toward Hick and asked, "And what did the letters contain?"

"Most of them contained what you would expect. Wishes for his family's welfare, lies about how decent he was being treated at the jail. But there was one in particular that caught my attention." Hick reached into his pocket and passed the note to Father Grant.

The priest read the letter and frowned. "And did she? Did Mrs. Delaney go to the prison?"

"Mrs. Delaney can't read. She never knew she was needed."

Father Grant's gaze rested on the note. Hick had trouble placing his age because his hair was still thick and dark but his face looked strained and old as if he'd seen more than he wanted to remember. The priest sighed. "I'm still unclear on how I can help you."

Hick turned his hands over, his empty palms emphasizing his lack of answers. "I was hoping the note might jolt your memory. Make you think of something that seemed out of place with Abner, something that didn't quite add up."

Father Grant stared at the letter in his hand. Shaking his head, he told Hick, "I wrote so many of these. Few of the men at that prison could read or write." He stared at it, contemplating the words.

Hick leaned forward. "I know it seems crazy to drive all the way out here, but if them boys is innocent I'll do anything to keep them out of that prison farm. I know what goes on there."

The last bit of reserve seemed to flow out of the priest. His eyes narrowed and the corners of his mouth turned down. "You know what goes on there. The whole world knows what goes on there and not one person raises a finger to stop it." He motioned toward the mounds of papers. "These papers are notes I took while I served there. Notes on the treatment of the prisoners, notes on the prisoners themselves, how many were poor, illiterate, Negro. They all say they're innocent, but some truly were." He paused and whispered as if he was alone with his thoughts. "Some truly were."

"I don't reckon you'd recall one man or why it was you seemed to think Abner was innocent or why you thought the investigation was flawed?"

"No I wouldn't," Father Grant said reaching behind him and refilling the glass. "That's why I kept these notes. There were just so many …" His voice trailed off and he closed his eyes. "Someday we may have a governor who gives a damn about these people and when we do, he'll read about this. About the torture and the suffering. About the cruelty."

Hick's shoulders sagged in discouragement. "I don't reckon it's an easy task to go through all that and find notes on a specific person. Something that might help me?"

The priest picked up the glass and stared at the liquid. He set it down without taking a drink and ran his hand through his hair. Looking at the stacks and stacks of file folders around him, he replied, "These folders are the last days of the lives of men, men made in the image and likeness of God, but who were treated like brutes. They are their last thoughts, their hopes for their loved ones, their regrets. They aren't things to be passed around."

"But if Abner were alive, he'd do anything to save his children, to keep them out of that place. You must know that."

"That may be true," Father Grant agreed, "but to find the file on one man, out of the thousands in here"—the priest looked around the room—"that's nigh on impossible."

So the trip was made in vain after all. Hick slumped back in his chair and shook his head. Father Grant regarded him silently for a moment and then said, "I've been a priest for sixteen years. My first assignment was that prison farm. I used to believe that men were basically good until I went there." The ice cubes tinkled in his glass as he took a drink and sat it back down with a emphatic thud. "That six years was my trial by fire. It wasn't so much what I saw as what I didn't see. I didn't see any outcry from the public. I didn't see anyone pretend to care about the suffering that went on behind those bars. I didn't see any compassion … all I saw was slavery by another name."

Hick's eyes fixed on the white collar showing above Grant's black shirt. "Why were you sent to that prison anyway?"

Father Grant smiled a bitter smile. "Less than two percent of this state is Catholic. You know how many Catholics I met in that prison? Zero. Not one. But those men needed comfort, they needed to know that God was still in heaven, and that He cared even if people here on earth seemed to have forgotten them. There was only one reason a Catholic priest was sent to that prison. Let's just say the local ministers didn't want to sully their hands working with poor folks and Negroes.

Hick sighed and rose to leave. "Well, I appreciate you seeing me."

"You know you're the first cop to come into this office without a warrant to haul off one of my parishioners?" Father Grant said, rising from his chair for the first time and holding out a hand. "Our local sheriff takes great delight in hauling my people off to jail."

Hick frowned. "Yes, I'm acquainted with him."

"It was good of you to drive this far to help those boys. There aren't many who'd take the time."

Hick shrugged. "I told their mama I'd do all I could. They're good boys and all she's got for support. I don't know how any of them will make it if they're arrested."

The priest towered over him and his dark eyes held a deep sadness. "As long as you treat men like animals, they're going to act like animals. The Pinewood Prison Farm is the kind of place where good men come out bad and bad men come out worse." He paused as some emotion seemed to well up in him. "Those boys will be another story in a litany of sad stories. That place is the closest thing to Hell on earth

I can imagine, filled with young boys, grey-haired grandfathers, even lunatics. I could say many of them didn't belong there, but no one belonged there. Some just seemed to get along better in that environment than others ... to prosper, even ... like they were born to brutalize."

A shiver went down Hick's spine. He shook his head. "Eben and Jed Delaney are good boys. Always out, looking for food ... or work. Anything to help their mama and their little sister and brother." He pursed his lips in anger. "Just damned bad luck, and I don't know what I can do to help them."

The priest reached down and picked up a small notebook and a pen. "What did you say the man's name was?"

"Delaney. Abner Delaney."

He finished writing and looked up. "You see the mess I have ... I'll do my best, but I can't make any promises."

"I wouldn't ask you to," Hick answered, "but I appreciate anything you can do."

The men shook hands and Hick walked out the door, carefully closing it behind him. The secretary had evidently been asked to wait and she told Hick, "The storm ain't so bad now."

Hick looked out the window and saw that it was barely raining. The woman had a nameplate on her desk that read 'Esther Burton'. "Excuse me, Miss Esther, but may I use your phone?"

She looked doubtful. "Ain't it long distance?"

"I'll reverse the charges."

Assured, she handed him the phone and Hick called the

office, getting Adam on the phone. "Yeah, I'm still in Broken Creek," he said. "Any news on the Delaney brothers?"

Esther Burton's face registered surprise as the receiver slipped from Hick's hand and landed with a clunk on the desk. Grabbing it back up, he spoke quickly. "What do you mean they weren't on Smitty's truck?"

8

"**S**on of a bitch," Hick grumbled as he put his coffee cup on the saucer with a bang.

"It seems the habitually inept law enforce-ment of the town of Cherokee Crossing has done it again. As of this printing two murder suspects, Jed and Eben Delaney, are on the lam. Sheriff Hick Blackburn was overheard by this reporter stating that in his 'learned' opinion the young miscreants were innocent and flatly refused to bring them in. As their flight from Cherokee Crossing has made their guilt evident it is hoped that Sheriff Blackburn can redeem himself with a quick apprehension before they kill again."

Hick closed the newspaper. He had slept little and risen early after his unsuccessful trip to Broken Creek. The last thing he wanted to deal with was Wayne Murphy's nonsense. Maggie looked up from the pile of diapers she was folding.

"What's wrong?"

"Damned Murphy."

"Now what?"

Hick handed her the paper and watched the color in her cheeks rise. She handed the paper back and told him, "Nobody believes a word he writes."

"That may or may not be true, but I hate how he twists everything to sell his papers." Wayne Murphy had long been Hick Blackburn's nemesis. Things had gone from bad to worse when Hick refused to let Murphy accompany him to Claire Thompson's arrest for the murder of an infant two years earlier, arguably the biggest thing to happen in Cherokee Crossing's history. Murphy used the paper often to exercise his vindictiveness.

"Wayne Murphy isn't likely to change, you know that. So no use worrying over him." Maggie said grabbing another diaper. She folded the last one and stretched. "I best get Jimmy ready for church. You goin'?"

He shook his head. He hadn't gone in a while but Maggie asked every week nonetheless. "Not this week. Not with everything I've got to do."

"I'll go by for your mama again," Maggie told him. "She don't need to be walkin' in this heat."

"Thanks," Hick replied. He rose from the chair and grabbed his hat. He had a long day of investigating ahead.

"Don't forget, Tobe and Fay are coming for Sunday dinner," Maggie called after him.

Hick had forgotten, and he could tell Maggie knew it. Gladys' murder was hanging heavily on him and he had a lot of do. The idea of entertaining guests was unappealing. When things were bad at work, the tension always spilled over at home.

"I'll be here," he promised.

Frustration boiled within him as he drove to work. He was annoyed with himself for, once again, letting Wayne Murphy get under his skin, and he felt ashamed for getting so wrapped up in work that home felt like an inconvenience. To not invite Tobe and Fay when they were in town was really not an option, and yet he was still irrationally angry with Maggie for doing it.

Tobe had been Hick's best friend in high school and together the two boys had been summoned to war. Though not casualties in body, both men had been scarred and wounded by their experiences in Europe. Tobe found solace in a bottle and had ultimately carved out a shaky personal armistice by only indulging in his lust on the weekends. He and Fay moved to St. Louis where Tobe soberly worked at the Fisher body plant Monday through Friday, and stayed drunk from Friday night to Sunday. It hurt Hick to see his friend reduced to this and he was an unwelcome reminder of the war, a visual demonstration that their public personas belied secret, personal demons.

❧

Adam was seated at his desk, feet up and newspaper in hand, when Hick entered the station. "Any luck with the preacher?"

Hick hung his hat on the coat rack and shook his head. "He didn't remember Abner. Unfortunately, Abner's story is all too common."

"I was afraid of that," Adam studied Hick a moment. "You see any sign of Brewster?"

Hick shook his head. "I don't reckon he shows up on that side of town unless it's to serve a warrant."

"That's just what I'd expect from that bastard. Speaking of bastards …" He picked the paper back up and asked, "What the hell are we going to do about Murphy"

In spite of his calm appearance, Hick sensed the rage seething below Adam's controlled exterior.

"What can we do?" Before Hick made it to his desk, the station door burst open and the formidable presence of the Reverend Ted Wheeler filled the room.

With arms folded across his chest and a face seemingly carved from cold stone, Wheeler stared at the two men. "Well?"

"Well, what?"

"As a citizen of this town, I demand to know what you are doing to apprehend those two murderers."

Hick lowered himself into his chair, and fought to keep his voice controlled, measured. "Who do you mean?"

The reverend strode across the room and slammed his fist down on Hick's desk. With menace in his narrowed eyes, he growled. "Don't play games with me. Gladys Kestrel was like family to you. Look how she cared for your father, and this is how you repay her? By letting her killers walk away scot free? Shame on you!"

Hick rose and looked Wheeler in the eye. "Let's get one thing straight, right now. Eben and Jed Delaney are not 'murderers' in any sense of the word. They may have been convicted already in Murphy's rag and in your mind, but they are innocent until proven otherwise. And furthermore, don't you tell me who to arrest or how to do my job. I don't want to hear any of your 'sins of the father' bullshit, and I don't want you spreading your hate through town. We've got Murphy to do that, we don't need two of you."

Reverend Wheeler's eyes widened and his mouth tightened. "How dare you? Do you know who you're talking to?"

"I'm talking to a man who ought to be preaching love, but who chooses to preach hate. That's normally not my business. Not unless it starts disturbing the town or interfering with an ongoing investigation."

The Reverend's eyes glimmered. "And if it does?"

"Murder ain't the only thing can get a man locked up."

"Are you threatening me?" Wheeler's voice was low.

"Advising you."

"I see."

"Don't you have a sermon you ought to be preachin' somewhere?" Adam said.

Wheeler's face contorted with fury as he spun toward Adam who now had his newspaper rolled up in his hands as if he were going to swat a fly. "Oh, I've got a sermon alright." Wheeler spat the words. "I've got a sermon and it's not about God's love. God is a God of vengeance as well." He walked back to the door, shoulders straight and head high as if he were in a military parade. He turned and cast a wrathful eye upon Hick and Adam. "I should have known better than to think anything would be accomplished by my coming here. It appears going out after those boys might be more work than you're accustomed to." He looked pointedly at Adam's feet on his desk before turning to leave.

"He's gonna be a problem," Adam said nonchalantly after the door slammed.

"He is a problem," Hick corrected. "Everyone knows Murphy's full of shit, but people will start believin' Wheeler. We've got to find those boys, fast. Where could they have gotten to?"

"They could be anyplace there's work to be found," Adam replied. "They could be in Illinois or Michigan. Hell, they could be all the way out to California."

"I reckon I'll need to find out if Miss Delaney's had any word."

"Let's hope she has. Them disappearing like this only adds fuel to Wheeler's fire."

"Wheeler," Hick repeated. "Wheeler and Murphy, they're like kings of their own little kingdoms with no idea of what goes on in the world outside of their realm. They think they have all the answers. Hell, Jed and Eben have never even been in trouble. Not once."

"Neither had Abner," Adam reminded Hick. "And, yet, he was convicted of first degree murder."

"I'm not buying it," Hick responded. "What possible motive would those boys have had to kill Gladys."

Adam looked at the stacks of letters they had brought from Gladys' room. "Maybe something in here will give us an idea." He opened one and began scanning it.

Hick settled back onto his chair and examined Abner Delaney's letters. "Or something in here," he said, opening the next envelope on the stack..

The clock ticked as Hick read letter after letter from Pinewood Prison, each like the other. Abner worried over his family's welfare, while doing nothing to save himself. There was never any suggestion that Abner thought of filing an appeal. Just a constant stream of hopes for a better future for his children.

Hick ran his hand through his hair in frustration. His thoughts swirled and in his mind, he saw Gladys's torn face and the earnest expressions of Jed and Eben. He saw Pearl Delaney's haunted eyes and the wistful longing of Mourning. He played every scenario over and over in his head and none of them pointed to the Delaney brothers as possible killers. And yet, they were the ones who had stumbled upon Gladys's body, they were the ones who lost a father in prison for a killing in which Gladys seemed to have taken an interest, and they were the ones everyone in town suspected. Anger welled up again as he thought of the hatred and vengeance Wayne Murphy and Ted Wheeler were stirring up.

He scooted his chair back abruptly. "I need some air," he muttered and walked outside. He paused in front of the station and flipped open his lighter, turning the thumbwheel, lighting the wick. He flipped the lid closed and popped it back open, repeating the motion, staring absentmindedly into the distance. He knew enough about the Pinewood Prison Farm to understand just how much information

Abner withheld from his family. He knew Abner would have been subjected to hours of grueling work in the hot sun, picking cotton, and would have likely been beaten. He knew prisoners were routinely tortured and not fed properly. He knew of the brutality of the prison trustees, hardened criminals given authority to exercise justice, or vengeance, without impunity. He lit a cigarette and took a long draw letting the smoke slowly seep out his nostrils. "Why wouldn't Abner fight to get away from there?"

"Uncle Hick!" a voice shouted, cutting through Hick's thoughts. He turned to see Benji, Adam's oldest son, and Jack Thompson walking with the two Shelley girls.

"What are ya'll up to?" Hick asked, tossing the cigarette to the ground and crushing it.

"You remember Lucille and Edna?" Benji asked. Benji, a smaller version of Adam, was tall for his age and looked to be the same age as Lucille Shelley, although in reality he was only eleven and Lucille, fourteen.

"I remember them when they were little girls. I don't recognize them now," Hick replied with a smile.

"Miss Pam says we're to entertain them," Jack announced. Jack Thompson was one of Adam and Pam's foster sons.

"Is that a fact?" Hick said, putting his lighter in his pocket. "What do ya'll have planned?"

"We're going to the diner for a Coke," Benji replied importantly.

"Daddy had to go back to work," Edna piped. The youngest Shelley girl was small like her mother with two blonde Shirley Temple pigtails.

"My daddy was a principal, too," Hick said. "I remember him working all summer long while us kids had time to play."

"Mama begged him to let us stay a little longer so we could do some visiting. We're staying at your old house," Lucille told him. She was slender with her father's good looks and her mother's expressive eyes.

"Good," Hick told her. "My mama likes company."

Benji cleared his throat. "Uncle Hick, we're kinda getting thirsty."

Hick nodded and said, "Ya'll have fun. Don't throw your Coke bottles in the ditch."

"We won't," Benji called as they ran down the street, their laughter a stark contrast to the pall that hung over the town. It was more than the usual Sunday quiet. It was a wariness, sprung from the knowledge that one of their most beloved citizens had been brutally murdered. The usual sounds seemed hushed and shrouded in the awe that a tragic and premature death creates.

Hick was ten years old when Susie Wheeler was murdered. It seemed funny that he did not remember the event. He did not remember if his parents talked about it—they must have—or what was written in the paper. But he remembered the feeling, this feeling, that something terrible had happened and nobody could explain it or make it right. He and Tobe had been running down the street, shouting at the top of their lungs when the door to the post office opened and Mrs. Benson, Maggie's mother, had stepped out. She caught the boys by their arms and whispered kindly to them, "Don't shout so boys. Today is a day of respect."

The awful silence. That was the only thing he remembered about Susie Wheeler's death and the only thing he remembered four months later when Ronnie Pringle died. It was as if the town had been collectively punched in the gut. But Ronnie died in June and by July Hick, Tobe, and the rest of the boys were back at the ball field. Death's bony fingers released the town but stayed wrapped around the throats of those it hurt the most.

The door to the station opened and Adam stepped out. "Got a call from Miss Barnes. She says she spied Eben Delaney in the cotton patch. I'm goin' to head out there and try and calm her down."

"Can you stop by the Delaneys and find out if Miss Delaney's got any word?"

Adam nodded and strode to the squad car.

"If anything turns up, come on out to the house. I reckon Tobe will be passed out by eight o'clock anyway," Hick called after him.

∾

Hick's prediction had been pretty accurate. Tobe had arrived tipsy and the five beers he drank at dinner had mellowed him to the point that he fell asleep on the porch swing before the lightning bugs began to flicker. As Tobe snored, Hick, Maggie, and Fay enjoyed strawberry shortcake and coffee.

"Maggie, this is delicious." Fay licked her spoon and dug in for another bite. "The strawberries in St. Louis don't have the tartness ours do. They taste old."

Hick motioned outside toward the porch swing. "He getting by okay at work?"

Fay nodded. "They like him a lot. He's a good worker, and the foreman says he might get promoted to the paint department. Painting cars pays better than putting in windshields."

"How's Bobby like his school?" Maggie asked.

"He likes it and is doing well." Fay set her plate down and sipped her coffee. "He's got a nice group of boys he plays with. I mean it ain't like here where we had nature and the swamp and Jenny Slough. He's got alleys and amusement parks and swimming pools."

"I miss that slough," Hick said. "Fishing the levees and ditches ain't the same. There's no mystery, no cypress trees. It's hot and sunny and dull."

"It was a shame they dammed it up," Fay agreed. "I remember growing up out there and how mysterious the world seemed. We had our own cast of characters, that's for sure. We had the threat of the spooky eephus to make us behave and Miss Delaney's potions to keep us healthy."

The name of Pearl Delaney brought up unwanted associations with work and Hick pointedly put them out of his mind.

"And Johnny," he added.

"Oh, Coal Oil Johnny! Whatever happened to him?"

"He and Patsy the Mule just disappeared when they dammed the slough. No one's seen hide nor hair since."

A loud snort and groan from the porch reminded them of Tobe's presence. Fay shook her head. "It's a shame Miss

Delaney don't have a potion for that."

"What kind of potions did Miss Delaney give you?" Maggie asked.

"Well, if you ask me they weren't anything but coal oil with a little molasses. You town kids had Doc Prescott to doctor you up. We had Miss Delaney's snake oil. She could cure everything from the croup to malaria."

"I think I'd rather have malaria." Maggie shuddered.

"Bless her heart, but Miss Delaney sure tried to help people out. They were good people. No one who knew him ever believed Abner done that to Susie Wheeler. Most thought it was her fellow, Ronnie."

A slow ache took hold at the base of Hick's skull. He wanted to forget about work, not discuss it over dessert. Maggie glanced over at him, then quickly turned the conversation to the latest gossip around town. Hick took advantage of the moment to step out onto the porch and light a cigarette. Tobe snorted once again and opened his eyes.

He straightened up and patted the swing. "Hey Hick," he said with a slur. "Have a seat, buddy."

Hick settled in and offered his friend a cigarette.

Tobe shook his head. "One vice is about all I can afford."

Hick took a long draw feeling the comforting smoke warm his lungs. He exhaled and the two men sat silently on the porch swing, the sounds of frogs and crickets filling the air around them.

"How's St. Louis treating you?" Hick finally asked.

"Shit, it's hotter than hell in that factory and the houses are on top of each other. Still, there's a good tavern at the end of the street and they let Bobby run me home a bucket of beer a couple of times a night on the weekends." He shrugged. "I got beer, work, baseball, and Fay. And Bobby. I guess it's alright."

Hick leaned back against the swing, took another deep drag, and peered off into the darkened distance.

"What about you?" Tobe asked. "You doin' okay?"

Hick shrugged. "Yeah. Mag works her ass off around here, and it feels like I'm never around."

"Ya'll should come on up some weekend," Tobe urged. "Come to a Cardinals game at Sportsman's. I take Bobby up there some Sundays and we watch Slaughter and Musial and Schoendeist. It's the next best thing to playin'."

"That'd be nice. Maybe when Jimmy's older."

They sat in silence listening to the swing creak and the night gather around them. "Listen, Hick," Tobe said finally, "if you and Maggie ever decide to get out of this place, I can get you on at Fisher or if not there, Chevrolet is hiring. Union wages, good benefits. You wouldn't have to put up with the shit you put up with here."

Surprised, Hick turned to look at Tobe. "I'm—"

"I know what goes on here and how this place treats you." He leaned forward and looked into Hick's face. "Don't let them suffocate you. You ever need me, you know I got your back. Think about this, in the city I'm just another factory worker. Nobody knows who I am ... or what I've done." The old sadness was there, a weight Tobe just couldn't set aside. Hick saw it and Tobe knew he saw it. But neither man wanted to grapple with it, so Tobe quickly reached into the cooler for another beer and offered Hick one. Hick didn't say no, so Tobe opened them both, took a drink from his, and sank back onto the swing. "It's good to be anonymous." There was unmistakable relief in his voice. "You ever get tired of it all, you just give me a call. Life is good in the city."

9

"The Methodists are riled up this morning," Adam commented as he slid into the booth across from Hick. The diner was packed for a Monday morning, and there had been more than a few angry glances Hick's way.

Hick stuffed the United Auto Workers pamphlet Tobe had given him in his shirt pocket and took a drink of coffee. "Sounds like Wheeler gave it to 'em good yesterday. 'Vengeance is mine' and all that."

"He's gonna be a problem," Adam said for what Hick thought might be the hundredth time.

Hick nodded, signaling the waitress for a refill. After Tobe and Fay left the house, he had worked the night shift and now felt bleary-eyed and exhausted after several sleepless nights.

The door to the diner opened and Elizabeth Shelley approached their booth. "May I join you?"

Adam slid over and made room for her.

"How's my mama doin' today?" Hick asked Elizabeth.

"She's so sweet takin' us in. I sure appreciate her putting us up for a few days," Elizabeth said as Shirley Daniels came by, filled her coffee cup, and set down a new container of cream and a bowl of sugar. "George needed to get back to work, but the girls wanted to stay and visit with some of their friends. They like Tennessee all right, but this still feels like home."

"I know Mama enjoys the company."

"I haven't had a chance to tell you, but your little boy is adorable." Elizabeth poured cream and sugar in her coffee and stirred it absently. "I can scarcely believe you're married with a child. I remember you as a kid who was always in trouble and now you've got your own baby and you're the sheriff."

Hick blushed. "I do my best to stay away from trouble now."

The door to the diner clanged open and Wayne Murphy walked in. He paused at the booth and sneered, "I see you boys are working hard again."

Elizabeth Shelley's eyes narrowed. "Your piece this morning on hogs was inspired, Wayne. They seem to be a subject you really understand."

"Ha ha," he answered before positioning himself at a booth in the back of the diner, a convenient place to study everything around him.

Elizabeth shook her head. "I suppose it's not always easy being sheriff. I read in the paper that Jed and Eben Delaney are actually suspects now. I can hardly believe it."

"They're not. We haven't formally named any suspects. That's Wayne Murphy's doing. He's the judge and jury of Cherokee Crossing, Arkansas."

"He hasn't changed. Other than finding poor Gladys, what possible reason does Murphy have to think the Delaney brothers killed her?"

"Oh, you know this town," Adam answered. "The Delaneys are an easy target. They're poor and uneducated and people don't trust what they don't understand."

"So you don't think they did it." She looked from Adam to Hick.

"We really don't know," Hick admitted.

"I'm a little relieved," Elizabeth said looking up from her coffee cup. "They're the type that usually get blamed and sent away. It's good to see you having an open mind. But if not the Delaneys, then who?"

"We have no idea. Honestly, none of it makes sense. Gladys didn't have an enemy in this world."

"That's just what George and I said. It had to be someone who didn't know her because everyone who knew her loved her and would never dream of hurting her."

Shirley came by with Adam's breakfast and to refill everyone's coffee. Hick took a drink and then began, "I tell you, there's something off about this whole ..." His thought was interrupted when he saw Wash hurrying across the street.

Wash pushed through the door with a jangle and headed straight to Hick's booth. "Sheriff, got a call from that Preacher up to Broken Creek. Wants you to come back 'cause he found what he was looking for."

Noticing Murphy sit up straighter, Hick rose slowly, swallowing the last of the liquid from his cup. "Keep your voice down, Wash." He turned to Adam and whispered, "I'm headed up there now. The quicker we get this thing figured out, the better."

"You okay driving after staying up all night?" Adam asked.

"It's not that far."

"Broken Creek?" Elizabeth asked. "What on earth are you going there for?"

"Hopefully, some answers." Hick grabbed his hat, then stopped.

Adam nodded, and glanced back at Murphy. "Walk out of here slow and quiet-like. I'll keep a lid on Murphy."

Hick threw some coins on the table. "Thanks."

Wash followed Hick out into the sunshine. "Sheriff, before you leave can I have a word?"

"Sure," Hick noted the worried look on Wash's face. "What's on your mind?"

Wash nodded toward the station and the two men stepped inside. The chaos of paperwork that littered the three desks made Hick uneasy about leaving. Seemed like they'd never get through all the files and letters. He glanced at Wash. The older man's hands were shaking and he pulled a handkerchief from his pocket and ran it across his head.

"Sheriff, I'm needin' to ease my mind."

"Sit down, Wash. What's the matter?"

Wash sank into a chair in front of Hick's desk. "It's Abner Delaney," he said.

Hick sat behind his own desk and leaned forward. "What about Abner?"

"I was there when the posse brought him in. He was sittin' at home eating his dinner when it happened. I always did think it odd he wasn't hidin' out somewhere."

Hick nodded and Wash continued. "You know it never occurred to me to even think Abner wasn't our man. Sheriff Michaels, he was convinced of it the minute Abner wandered into the station that day and told us he'd found a body. Michaels never really considered anyone else. And then there was Wheeler."

"Wheeler?"

Wash shook his head. "He was beside himself with rage. He came in here demanding Roy lock Abner up, and Wheeler's a man used to getting his way. I don't reckon Roy thought Abner Delaney was worth getting Wheeler riled up over."

Hick's heart pounded and a bead of sweat rolled down his back. Wash fidgeted in his seat and Hick offered him a cigarette. He declined, but Hick took one and put it between lips so dry the paper stuck to them. Wash looked down at his feet. "I guess I reckoned it would all get straightened out in court. But it didn't, and it really didn't seem to matter. You know, when Michaels was sheriff things was different around here. Michaels always said his job was to keep the peace."

Hick lit his cigarette and looked into Wash's face. "Well, ain't that what we're doin'?"

Wash drew in a deep breath and managed a weak smile.

"Maybe. But Michaels was more concerned with keepin' the town happy and calm. He'd of already brought them boys in."

Hick kept his voice steady. "You think I should have done that?"

Wash wiped the back of his hand over his mouth. "No, Sheriff, I don't. You're a different man than Roy Michaels. I reckon there's a difference between keepin' the peace and finding justice." He glanced up and held Hick's gaze. "I'm thinkin' now we done Abner wrong, and I didn't have the sense to see it then. Never even thought about it much until now.."

Hick watched as tears formed in Wash Metcalfe's eyes. "I just done what I thought was right," the deputy said in a tired voice. He closed his eyes and shook his head.

At home, Maggie stood in the bedroom doorway with the expression Hick had come to know so well. She would never interfere with his job, never tell him she was unhappy with anything he was doing. But she could never hide what was on her mind. Even now, the slight line between her eyebrows testified to her discomfort with him going back to Broken Creek, Arkansas.

Hick tore off his shirt and threw it on the bed, hurriedly slipping into a clean uniform. "I'll be fine."

"But you've been up all night," she protested. "Why don't you just lie down for a couple of hours?"

"You haven't seen what Wheeler and Murphy are doing to this town. The quicker we get this figured out, the quicker things can get back to normal."

He finished buttoning his shirt and faced her. "I'll be back soon."

She nodded. "Alright. Please be careful. If you get tired, pull over."

"I just had my fill of diner coffee so I ought to be fine."

He headed through the doorway into the kitchen and grabbed the old thermos from the counter. He poured it full of yet more coffee and started out the door.

"Hickory."

He turned.

"You forgot to kiss me goodbye." There was an unmistakable note of sadness in her voice.

He crossed the room and held her close as a wave of guilt washed over him. She had been neglected and he knew it. He put his finger under her chin and tilted her face toward him. "I'm sorry," he told her meeting her gaze. "I don't know why I get this way." He kissed her and felt her pain. "I'm sorry."

She forced a smile. "It's fine. You know I love you."

"Yeah. I know you do. And you know I love you. More than anything. But I've gotta go do this."

She nodded.

He paused at the door. "Don't forget to lock everything up behind me."

As he pulled onto the county road, he removed his hat and lit a cigarette. The vision of Maggie's tired, sad face was before him as he drove. "You know I love you," she had said. Why she loved him was the big question of his life. He was reserved and aloof. He held his cards close to his chest and all of the female patience and love in the world would never change that. But Maggie had known all this. She had known it for years—since they were kids—and she knew the war had made it worse. And yet, she loved him anyway, and she was the only woman he could ever love. But her loyalty and steadfastness was a mystery he could never solve.

The Church of Our Lady of Sorrows in Broken Creek, Arkansas looked less dismal in the sunshine. The puddles of water that had been standing all over the gravel lot were gone and a pleasant breeze twirled through the orange day-lilies blooming beside the steps.

The young woman in the outer room was not there when Hick arrived at the church office. In her place sat the priest, Father Grant, in khaki trousers and a Pendleton shirt with his legs stretched out in front of him.

"You didn't waste much time," he remarked, rising and moving toward his office.

"The boys have gone missing, and I'm afraid if they turn back up I'm gonna have a riot on my hands."

"I see," Grant said without surprise. "Well, come on."

Hick followed Father Grant into his office which seemed to be in an even worse state of disarray than before. The radio was playing softly in the corner and the priest paused to sip some coffee. "Mondays are my day off," he explained. "I have been trying to make some sense of all this." His eyes lingered on the stacks of paper and for a moment he seemed lost. "Please have a seat."

Hick sat down and was surprised to see the typewriter uncovered and a sheet of paper sticking out of it. The stacks of folders nearby were straightened and appeared to have been organized.

Father Grant picked up an accordion file and held it up. "This is the last year of Abner Delaney's life. I've been re-reading these," he said indicating the clutter of folders all around him. "It's pretty grim fare." He sat down at his desk and his dark eyes studied Hick. "You know, when I first got out of the seminary I thought my belief in some sort of innate goodness in man was essential for my survival ... but as you see, I'm still breathing. In the sixteen years I've been a priest I have never once lost my faith in God. It's man I no longer believe in."

"I don't understand ..." Hick began but Father Grant interrupted him.

"Pinewood Prison Farm is what the world becomes with-out God. It is a place where the strong and the powerful prey upon the weak and the old. I watched guards caress their wives with the same hands they used to slap old men working in cotton fields. I watched church going men abuse and torture the powerless, the illiterate, the defenseless and all the while they were crucifying Jesus again. The power-ful denied the powerless their humanity because they were convicts and forgot that Jesus was crucified as a criminal."

He studied the file folder, and Hick waited for him to continue. "After you left, I started digging through these files. I decided I'd search for that folder as long as there was some hope it could help those boys. And as I opened the folders, the faces stared up at me. Picture after picture, men who had been executed and thrown into unmarked graves, and I knew then it was my duty to expose their sufferings or the world would never know what happened. I have decided to write a report for Governor McGrath. At least he pretends to care." Father Grant leaned forward and regarded Hick. "Do you believe in God?"

"What?"

"When I found that folder, it seemed to me like it had to be for a reason. That's why I wonder if you believe in God."

"Reverend, I was in the war, and I did a lot of things I'm ashamed of. I saw a lot of people die who shouldn't have, and I've spent a lot of time mad as hell that God let it happen. I can't say I don't believe. I just don't know what good it's done me."

"What has God to do with war? God didn't start that war."

"But He turned away. He didn't care."

"Did He turn away? Or did He weep at the mess we'd made? It's a mistake to think that because bad things happen God isn't there or doesn't care. God didn't create man for savagery; he didn't create us to kill. We do that to ourselves when we choose fear over love."

"And what happens to us when we make these choices? At what point is it just too late?"

"No one is irredeemable. You are still capable of doing noble things, regardless of what you've seen or done. The fact that you drove out here not once, but twice, to help those boys shows me there is a lot of good in you. You can make this right for them." His eyes met Hick's. "You can show me. Help restore my faith in the goodness of men."

Images exploded in Hick's mind. He saw Claire Thompson's face as he arrested her. He saw her lack of remorse. He saw Ted Wheeler's face contorted with anger and Wayne Murphy's scornful gaze. But he remembered the touch of Maggie's hands on his face the day she reminded him that he was more than one event ... more than one catastrophic mistake. There was bad in the world, but there was good, too. He looked up and met the eyes of Reverend Jefferson Davis Grant, a man who needed to remember the good as well. "I'll try. I'll do my best by them boys."

Father Grant nodded. "I know you will. Believe me, that's more than most would do." He regarded the folder in his hand. "Well, I know you didn't drive this far to hear me go on and on." Grant reached over the desk and handed the folder to Hick.

Hick was surprised at the weight in his hand. "When you found this ... did anything come back to you? Do you remember anything about Abner?"

"I'm sorry to say that I don't. I saw so many go through that place. But as you can see I took notes. Lots of notes." He picked up his coffee cup and shut off the radio. After a moment he said, "You know, I've never given one of these files to anyone. Never let anyone else read a single page. It seemed a betrayal of confidence, if you know what I mean. But I know the heart of a father. I may not have my own children, but the people of this church are my children. They are poor, they are Negro, and most are uneducated. The scale of justice is weighted against them, and as a father there is nothing I wouldn't do to protect them. In this instance, I think Abner Delaney, whoever he was, would do anything to protect his boys. Are you a father, Sheriff?"

"I am. A son. He's five months old."

"So you know." Father Grant searched Hick's face and then, as if finally satisfied, he nodded. "Take the file. And God help you."

Father Grant stood and walked out, leaving Hick sitting alone in his office. After a moment of stunned silence Hick rose to leave. As he stepped out into the entry way he spied the priest in the sanctuary. Father Grant did not turn when he heard Hick leave the office, and Hick left him kneeling before the altar.

The sunshine had the heightened brightness of an impending storm and the humidity was oppressive as Hick left the church. Squinting against the glare, he stood beside the car and lit a cigarette, unbuttoning the top button of his shirt.

"Well, who have we got here?" a voice chuckled behind him.

Hick turned to see Sheriff Earl Brewster walking across the parking lot toward him. "Shit," he thought, tossing the cigarette to the ground and meeting Brewster half-way. "Sheriff," Hick said, nodding, without holding out his hand.

Brewster regarded him and asked, "Boy, what in the hell are you doing in my town?"

"Here on business," Hick replied.

"You lookin' for one of these people? If you are, that Papist ain't gonna be no help. Shit, he coddles 'em like they're a bunch of damned babies."

Hick forced himself to keep his face relaxed, his voice even. "No, I'm not here to serve a warrant. Just lookin' for information ... old information."

Brewster tilted his head. "Information, huh? Tell me about it, son. Maybe I can help."

The word "son" coming from Brewster's mouth made Hick's stomach tighten and a hard lump caught in his throat. "No, thanks," he said. "I got what I need."

Brewster considered Hick, looking him up and down. "Maybe you could use some professional help ... or advice. I hear you got a stiff in Cherokee and some trash on the loose. I got friends who could round them boys up, and by the time they got back to Cherokee they'd be a lot smarter and a lot less inclined to run."

Hick's face grew taut at the word "stiff." His light eyes traveled up Brewster's bulky frame. They rested on his hardened face. Brewster spit tobacco juice on the church parking lot and grinned. "Just say the word, boy. Sometimes my friends like a little roughhousing, if you know what I mean."

"No," Hick said in a low, measured voice. "I don't need any help just now, but thank you anyway. I need to get back."

Brewster laughed, a hardened, mirthless laugh. "Jesus

Christ. No wonder you're here with the goddamned priest. You're as bad as he is. It never hurts to keep your boot on the necks of the trash. Keeps 'em from doin' exactly what they done in Cherokee. You'd better watch it, son, or your trash is gonna take over your town."

Hick closed his eyes and drew in a breath, waging war with his anger. When he opened his eyes, Brewster's mocking face was close to his. "Well, boy? What's it gonna be? You let me help you a little, and maybe I'll pretend you're an actual goddamned cop."

Hick stepped forward, refusing to be intimidated. "And maybe if you back off I'll pretend you're an actual human being."

Brewster's face grew red, but he burst out with laughter rather than rage. "What a pretty boy you are!" he bellowed. "Shit, I'm surprised Cherokee Crossing ain't been burnt to the ground by now. What do you do over there, invite the trash to the station for tea? Ya'll play patty-cake with 'em?" He laughed again, and coughed, spitting phlegm onto the gravel lot. "Jesus Christ, they must run right over you. I reckon they get away with murder!"

Hick did his best to appear unfazed. Looking Brewster in the eye he said, "To the best of my knowledge the only trash to get away with anything in Cherokee Crossing were kin of yours."

Brewster's mocking laughter ceased and his face darkened. "You got a lot to learn about how the law works in these parts, boy. A lot."

Hick shrugged. "The way it works in these parts ain't my

affair, and I don't give a shit how you and your boys conduct yourselves. The way it works in Cherokee Crossing is my way until I'm voted out."

Brewster laughed again and spat tobacco close to Hick's shoe. "Dumbass," he grumbled as he turned on his heel and walked back across the parking lot.

Hick watched Brewster pause beside his squad car and spit on the church parking lot again. Brewster glanced up and nodded at Hick and then got in the car and drove away.

When Brewster was out of sight, Hick jerked the car door open. "Goddamned son of a bitch!" He tossed the folder onto the seat beside him causing some of the pages to spill out. He reached over to shove them back into the file and saw Abner Delaney staring up at him. Hick picked up the photo. Abner was wearing the striped overalls, white denim shirt, and small cap that all the inmates wore. But as Hick stared, Abner's face seemed to come alive, his eyes beckoning, pleading with him, searching for something in Hick's own eyes much like Father Grant had. Abner's gaze bore through Hick like an awl through wood. "I'll do my best," Hick promised Abner in a voice thick with emotion. He placed the photo back in the file and put the car in gear. "Dammit, I'll do my best."

10

On the way back to Cherokee Crossing, the sky had grown darker and the oppressive heat and humidity signaled another storm brewing in the distance. By the time Hick pulled into the driveway, it was nearing dinner time and the house was a welcome sight after the long drive, the talk with Father Grant, and the confrontation with Brewster. Hick unlocked the kitchen door and was nearly undone with relief at seeing Maggie sitting at the table feeding Jimmy. It was so right. So normal. A man coming home to his wife and child, finding comfort in the joy of being loved … of just being home. He bent and kisssed the top of her head, but she didn't move or look at him.

"What's wrong?"

Maggie nodded toward the table. On it sat the United Auto Workers pamphlet. "Why do you have that, Hickory?"

Hick felt the heat rise to his cheeks. "Tobe gave it to me."

"But why do you have it? I can tell you've been reading it. Why?"

Hick sat the fat accordion file down and picked up the pamphlet. "Tobe said I should read it. And think about it. Said they need workers up in St. Louis at Chevrolet."

Maggie stared up at him. "And you were considering this without discussing it with me?"

"I hadn't gotten that far in my thinking."

"And my opinion … that doesn't matter? That doesn't figure in your thinking? That wouldn't have any weight in your decision?"

"Of course it would. If I thought it was a good opportunity, I would have talked with you."

"What about what I think?" Maggie put the bottle down and rose from the chair, unconsciously swaying where she stood. She placed Jimmy on her shoulders and patted his back. "Hickory, you don't talk to me … at all. About anything. How can I trust that you wouldn't just tell me one morning, 'We're going.'?" A small burp escaped the baby, and she placed him in the playpen, handed him a toy, then straightened up and looked Hick in the face. "I know there are things inside you that you can't put into words. Hurts, insecurities, fears … terrible things you have seen … I don't expect you to open all the darkness in your heart to me. I accept that and respect that there is part of you that you can never give to me. But, Hickory, when it comes to us, to our home and our family, you have to open up. I will never intrude upon your soul, but you can't lock me out of decisions that affect us all."

"I wouldn't lock—" Hick began, but Maggie interrupted.

"And by us all, Hickory, I mean all of us. You, me,

Jimmy, my mother, your mother. We have responsibilities here. Your mom isn't doing all that well. Now isn't the time to run out on her."

"My mom? What do you mean?"

Maggie stared at him. "Hickory, how can you not have noticed? She repeats herself, she forgets things. You haven't seen this?"

"I know mom's not as sharp as she used to be, but she's just getting older."

She shook her head. "It's more than that. Your sister and I have been talking about this for months. There's something more. You can't stay so wrapped up in work that you miss what's going on in your own family."

Hick sat wearily at the table. Had it been less than a week ago that Jake Prescott said the same thing to him? And yet, it seemed like an eternity. "You're right, Mag. I'm sorry."

Maggie held up the pamphlet. "What possessed you to consider this?"

"Don't you ever get tired of it all?" he said. "Tired of the politics and the Murphys and the gossip? Wouldn't it just be nice to be someplace where everyone doesn't know everything about you?"

She put her hands on his shoulder and rubbed his back. "I know this town hasn't been all that good to you. But there will always be bastards, wherever you go."

Maggie wasn't one to swear, and Hick couldn't help but smile up at her. He saw her eyes light on the accordion file folder. "Looks like you're planning to work tonight."

"Yeah."

"You worked all last night."

"I know, but this—"

"I know." She brought him a cup of coffee and sat down across from him. "Your dinner's in the oven. I'm going to take Jimmy to visit my mother. We'll get out of your way so you can get something done. I want you to find who really killed Gladys and why. And to help Eben and Jed. But more than that, I want you to know I believe in you." She rose to leave, but he grabbed her hand.

"Mag …"

She ran her thumb across the back of his hand and was quiet for a moment. "I know." She gave him a squeeze and stood. "I want to get over there before this storm hits, but I'll be back before too late."

He watched her pack a diaper bag and pick up Jimmy. "I'll be here," he promised.

The quiet settled around him after Maggie left. It was a much different house than the one he knew before getting married. Then, there had been clutter and grime and overflowing ashtrays. Now there was clutter of another sort—Jimmy's toys and Maggie's knitting, a pale pink nightgown hanging on the back of the bedroom door, photos and knickknacks that seemed to appear from nowhere. But despite all that, the house was neat and cheerful. He had moved to this small house at the edge of town right after the war in order to escape the fact that his father was no longer at home. The death of James Blackburn while Hick was away caused the old house to seem like foreign land and Hick could no longer stand being there. How did his mom cope? Surrounded by memory. Did she feel the strangeness of the place or had she grown accustomed to his father's absence? He thought about what Maggie had said. Was there something seriously wrong with his mom or were Pam and Maggie imagining things?

He rubbed his eyes, shook himself, and turned his attention to the folder in front of him.

Name: Abner Delaney, Age: 33 years, Nativity: Mississippi County, Arkansas, Conviction: Murder in the First Degree, Sentence: Death

Hick stared at the first page of the file. It seemed so sterile on paper, "Sentence: Death." And yet those cold words had changed the lives of all the Delaneys. The repercussions were well-known. Because her superstitious clientele was unlikely to cross a murdered spirit, Pearl Delaney lost the income she'd made from selling herbs and concoctions that were thought to cure a number of illnesses from constipation to consumption. Eben was four and Jed was three when their father was executed and they had never set foot in a schoolroom. As soon as they were able, they chopped firewood in the winter and picked cotton in the summer to make ends meet. They hunted, trapped, and fished. They grew up on the margins of civilization, doing what it took to survive and stay out of the poor house. The twins, Mourning and Job, were born while Abner was in prison. He never saw them.

Eben and Jed had been there for their mother. In spite of their youth they had stepped up and provided for the family. Matt Pringle vouched for the boys, and Hick knew he wasn't the only one to give them a good character reference. Lem Coleman had employed them every summer to chop the incessant weeds in his cotton fields. A twinge of guilt stabbed at him. Had he been a good son? Had he watched his mother fade without giving it a second thought?

He noticed when he came home from the war that she had lost interest in things she'd previously enjoyed. She still went to church, but was seldom out of the house other than Sunday. She let Pam get her groceries and rarely dressed in anything but a house coat. He had told himself she was just getting old. Was there more to it? He took another drink of coffee and pulled more papers out of the file.

Why would Abner Delaney kill Susie Wheeler? She was found fully clothed with no evidence of sexual assault, so it was not a crime of passion. Susie lived in town, Abner in the backwoods. They had probably never even met. Susie had no money and no money was found on Abner or any place in his cabin. What was his motive?

Hick quickly thumbed through the file and found scrawled notes on the trial. Although Father Grant hadn't been there, he had checked enough to know there had been problems.

It appears Abner Delaney's state appointed defense attorney is typical of those appointed to the indigent. Mr. Robert Dooley appears to have been intoxicated for much of the trial. He never cross examined a witness and never offered a defense. It seems Mr. Delaney's conviction was assured the day he was forced to admit he could not afford a lawyer.

Hick recalled Pearl Delaney telling him the same thing in her cabin and he thought of Wash's words at the station. It was clear Abner had received a raw deal. If he hadn't killed Susie, the state had executed an innocent man, a man whose only crime was being poor. And whose family had sunk even further into poverty after his death. But, if not Abner, who killed Susie Wheeler and what possible connection could there be between two crimes that were fourteen years apart? Hick took another gulp of coffee and stared at the heap of scrawled papers on the table. His shoulders slumped as he ran his hand across his chin. His mother had looked so tired at Gladys's funeral. She insisted she was okay, had repeated it over and over. But was she?

"Shit." He pushed the file away and stood up. Maggie's aim had hit its mark. He grabbed his raincoat, closed the door behind him, and headed toward his childhood home.

Maggie had taken the car, but the walk to his mother's house was short. The cotton fields across the road were beginning to bloom, the huge purple flowers searching for sun. Thunder cracked in the distance and tendrils of lightning unfolded across the distant sky. Hick hurried up the porch steps.

He opened the front door and called inside, "Ma?"

"I'm in here," she called from the kitchen.

Hick found her, as usual, dressed in an old house dress. She was peering out the window at the clouds. "Looks like another storm," she said with a note of fear.

"It's been one of those summers."

"Yes," she said a little dreamily. Then, as if finally realizing he was there she asked, "Have you had your dinner? Would you like some coffee?"

"I'm fine, Ma. Sit down."

She poured two cups and brought them to the table. "Would you like some cream?" she asked.

"Sure. That'd be nice."

She walked across the kitchen and paused in front of the ice box. She turned back to Hick and then opened the door, bringing out the pitcher of cream.

She sat down and raised her cup to her lips when a loud crash of thunder caused her to jump, spilling a little of the coffee onto the table. "My goodness," she laughed. "That startled me."

Hick watched her take a napkin and wipe up the coffee. She continued to wipe the table long after the coffee was gone.

"Where's Mrs. Shelley and the girls?" Hick asked.

His mother seemed confused for a moment and then answered, "Oh, George came by and picked them up this morning. Said he was lonesome." She smiled. "It was nice having them here. Such nice girls."

"I guess they kept you pretty busy."

"Oh, no." She waved his concern away. "The girls were barely here. They had a lot of visiting to do. Elizabeth was a help, though. She bought groceries and did a little light housekeeping for me."

A crack of lightning followed by the deep boom of thunder rattled the window frames. The rain fell suddenly, in heavy gray sheets. "Glad I made it before it started." Hick rose from the table and moved around the house closing windows. He heard his mother clear the coffee cups and run water in the sink, busying herself with the dishes. He opened the door to his room. It was the same as the day he'd left for the war. Just as Pam's was the same as the day she left to become Adam's wife. Two eternal shrines their mother could never dismantle.

From his bedroom window he could see his car next door at Maggie's old house and knew her visit there would outlast the storm. He pulled open the bottom drawer in his desk and smiled. His flashlight was still there. He picked it up and turned it on. Nothing. Unscrewing the end, he tipped it upside down. No batteries. He remembered waiting each night at bedtime for the signal. Three blinks always meant, "I love you, good night." How had it been possible that Magdalene Benson, the most beautiful girl he had ever seen, loved him and wanted him to know it? He still marveled at the very idea of it.

Restlessly, he wandered about the house, waiting for the storm to cease. He paused at the door to his father's study. As a child it was never good to be called into that room and, luckily, he had spent little time there. He walked inside expecting to find it untouched like the bedrooms. Instead, there were papers strewn over the desk and drawers hanging open.

"Ma?"

"Yes, Andrew?"

"Come here."

He heard the water turn off in the kitchen and listened to her shuffle through the house.

She stood in the doorway as if afraid to tread on hallowed ground.

"Have you been in here?" Hick asked in some surprise.

"Oh, no. Your father woudn't like it."

He stared for a moment. "Why is it such a mess?"

She entered the room and looked at the mess as if seeing it for the first time. Suddenly a light went on in her eyes. "Gladys left it like this."

"Wait, Gladys was here?" Stunned, Hick searched his mother's face. Had she just remembered?

"Oh, yes," she said. "She was here just the other day. Said she needed to look for something."

Hick was so shocked he couldn't think. "Ma, you didn't think you should tell me that?"

His mother's lips pursed and her brow drew together, the perfect picture of concentration.

"Did she find what she was looking for?"

"Oh, no," she said with certainty.

"How do you know?" Hick asked.

"Because when she left she told me she'd be back. She said if I didn't mind she wanted to look some more because she thought there might be something important in here."

"When was this exactly?"

"Oh it was just a few days ago. Just a couple of days before she … " Her face crumpled. "Oh, she's dead now. It was just a few days before she was found." Tears welled in her eyes.

Hick was dumbfounded. The rain was letting up and his mother walked to the front door to peer outside. He stood in the middle of his father's office and looked around him. Gladys must have been in a hurry, she was never one to leave things in a mess. "Ma, about what time was Gladys here?" he called.

Elsie appeared in the doorway. "It was early. I wasn't dressed."

Hick glanced at his mother's house dress, but said nothing. "You're sure it was early."

"Yes, Andrew. She got me out of bed."

"Did she tell you where she was going?"

"No. She said she'd just come from the school and she sat with me while I made coffee. But it wasn't like old times. She seemed jumpy and then asked to see your father's office, which was strange." She glanced in the room and shook her head. "I don't remember Gladys leaving it like this, but that's okay. She's family. I got no call to keep her out of there. She can look in there any time she likes, you tell her so."

Hick looked into his mother's eyes, the same blue eyes that had held the pain of a mother who had watched one son draw his last breath, and another march to war. She had watched cancer consume her husband and had witnessed all of life's sorrows and joys. Now those same eyes were slowly losing the ability to truly see.

He took his mother's hand and led her to the kitchen. "Can I get you some coffee?" he asked her, gently sitting her at the table.

"I'm okay." She smoothed her house dress and looked up at him.

He picked up a cup and crossed the room with the coffee pot in his hand. "Would you like some cream?"

She nodded and he opened the ice box and pulled out the pitcher. He sat it on the table beside the cup. "Have you had dinner?"

II

ick's mind spun as he drove his mother's car to the station. The revelation that Gladys Kestrel had been looking for something in his father's office jarred him. She hadn't found what she wanted and it appeared she left in a hurry. But what could she have been looking for? What connection did Hick's father have with any of this? He had searched through the papers scattered on the desk, but they offered no clues. Just old bills and mundane correspondence.

It was past six o'clock and Hick had not checked in at the station since returning from Broken Creek. He needed to talk with his deputies because none of this made sense. Adam's tense face greeted him as he walked through the door.

"This place has been a madhouse," Adam said as Hick hung his hat on the rack. "The phone hasn't stopped ringing. Wash is over at the Dolan's because they swear Eben Delaney is hiding out in their barn. Audie Briggs called, now convinced the Delaneys will kill her, too. Will Riley stopped by to give us a heads up. He's sold out of pistols and ammo and people are ordering in from other stores."

Hick shook his head. In four days, the peaceful town of Cherokee Crossing had become a wildfire of panic and hysteria, fueled by the greed of Wayne Murphy and the hate of Ted Wheeler.

Adam continued, "And that's not the worst of it." He picked up a pile of letters. "I've discovered something. It's not good. These are letters Susie Wheeler wrote to Gladys in February of 1936, a couple of weeks before her murder. Listen to this, '*Thank you for the advice. I had nowhere else to turn and I know you've been through this before*'." He picked up another letter and read, "*I will get the address in Memphis when the time comes to go there. I don't want it lying around the house for my father to find.*" He tossed the letter aside and picked up a third. "And this, '*I know you're right and I would have regretted it. I know this will be rough, but you've convinced me it's the right thing to do*'."

Silence filled the room. Hick stared at Adam.

Adam held up another letter. "I'm sure their opportunities to talk were limited. It's clear that whatever problem Gladys was helping Susie with was critical and Susie was so terrified of being found out that she couldn't bring herself to name it even in a private letter."

Hick sat down at his desk and put his head in his hands. "Jesus Christ."

"Appears Susie Wheeler was pregnant."

"Appears," Hick repeated. His mouth set in a thin line. "You know what that means?"

Adam nodded, his face grim. "Let's get Doc. We're gonna need his help."

∽

It was evening when the three men traveled up the driveway to the residence of Reverend Ted Wheeler. Fireflies had begun to wink from the tree line at the back of Wheeler's yard, and the air was finally cooling, the humidity mostly gone after the afternoon storm. The Wheeler house was a large, formidable brick structure, somewhat ostentatious for the town of Cherokee Crossing and second in size only to the dilapidated dwelling of Miss Audie Briggs. The three men strode across the lawn and climbed the wide steps to a large wraparound porch.

Their knock was answered by Mrs. Wheeler, a small, timid woman who had spent her life in the shadow of her husband. Smiling, she opened the door wide. "Won't you come in?"

The Reverend Wheeler entered the foyer from his study and regarded the men coolly. "I expect you have come to bring me good news?"

"Not exactly," Hick replied. "We need to speak with you in private."

"Can I get you gentlemen something to drink?" Mrs. Wheeler asked. "I just made a fresh pot of—"

"That won't be necessary," Wheeler interrupted.

Mrs. Wheeler looked surprised, but one glance from her husband sent her scurrying from the room.

"We can talk in my study," Wheeler said. They walked inside and he closed a set of white pocket doors behind him. Not inviting them to sit down, he took his place behind his desk, but remained standing. "Now what is it I can do for you gentlemen?"

Hick took a deep breath. "I'm not going to beat around the bush with you, Reverend. Did you know your daughter and Gladys Kestrel were corresponding quite extensively before Susie's murder?"

A hint of surprise flickered across his face, but his voice was flat, controlled. "I was not apprised of all of Susie's doings."

"But you kept a pretty close eye on her." Adam said.

The reverend's head swiveled toward Adam. "I did as any loving father would. May I ask where these questions regarding my poor Susie are leading? The child has been gone from this earth for fourteen years."

Hick glanced at Adam and Doc Prescott and back to Wheeler. "Reverend, we have reason to believe Susie was pregnant and was getting advice from Gladys Kestrel."

"Get out!" The command burst forth as a roar from somewhere deep within Wheeler's chest, bouncing off the walls, seething with barely controlled violence. His face was purple with rage, his eyes flashed fury, and his presence filled the room even though he had not moved from behind the desk. "How dare you come into my home with such lies, such slander. Get out or I'll throw you out!"

Hick's voice was calm, measured. "Here's how it's got to be … we need to exhume Susie's body. That's the only way we'll know for sure. We have good circumstantial evidence, but we want proof."

"What does any of this have to do with anything?" the Reverend demanded. "Because I criticize your lack of progress, you want to drag my daughter's reputation through the mud? By God I'll get a lawyer and sue you for all you're worth."

Hick tried to look unconcerned and continued as if Wheeler had never spoken. "There's two ways we can go about this. Doc's got an affidavit stating you and Mrs. Wheeler have decided to move Susie to another cemetery due to her headstone sinkin' in the sand. You sign it, we do the exhumation at night. Doc examines her while we send Murphy on a wild goose chase. She's back at the cemetery in the morning and nobody knows. Or, you fight this and we go and get a court order. Evidence may have been missed at the time of the burial, and that will be good enough for the judge. There's publicity, it will be in the paper and, if we're right about this, the world knows that Susie was pregnant when she was murdered. The choice is yours."

The Reverend appeared taken aback. He sank into his chair and regarded the three men before him with contempt. "What does this mean? Why does this matter … now? Why can't my daughter rest in peace?"

"Because Gladys seems to have taken a great interest in Susie's murder recently. Enough of an interest that it may have led to her own death."

"But there you have it! Abner Delaney's boys found out that Gladys was poking around and they shut her up."

"Does that make sense to you?" Adam stepped forward. "Their daddy is already dead. What would they have to gain?"

"For that matter, what did Abner Delaney have to gain from Susie's death in the first place?" Hick said.

Wheeler placed his hands flat on the desk as if ready to launch himself. He stared up at the three men with a sneer. "Now I suppose you're going to tell me Abner Delaney didn't kill Susie?"

"Think about it." Adam put an index finger to his temple. "Abner Delaney didn't know Susie. What was his motive?"

"His motive was his lack of concern for human life."

Hick shook his head. "I want you to stop and think about this. Set your hatred aside, Reverend Wheeler. Abner Delaney was respected by everyone he came into contact with. Someone who had never done as much as steal a loaf of bread. Someone who provided for his family in spite of ignorance and poverty, suddenly, inexplicably, murders your daughter in the woods? Does that make sense to you?"

"As if you can make sense of those people." Wheeler spat. "Violence runs in their blood."

"Did you follow Abner's trial?" Hick said.

"Of course I did. I was there every day looking at that animal who took my Susie's life. I was glad when they executed him. Glad. I would have pulled the switch myself."

"Did you notice that Abner's attorney never offered a defense?"

"What defense can you offer when your client is guilty as sin."

Hick closed his eyes and sighed, knowing full well there

was no convincing him. "You know, Roy Michaels only brought Abner in to shut you up. I don't intend to make that same mistake. I'll be damned if I tiptoe around you to keep you calm and quiet. The ball's in your court. What's it going to be?"

Wheeler stared up at the three men with hate in his eyes. "You still haven't told me what good digging up my poor child will do."

"Don't you get it?" Adam asked. "If Susie was pregnant, her baby had a father. That, in and of itself, would have been a motive."

It was clear the very thought of this was more than distasteful to Wheeler. He shuddered and the muscles along his jaw clenched and unclenched while Hick, Adam, and Doc waited. Finally Wheeler spoke. "Susie was seeing Ronnie Pringle. They courted right here in my parlor. How can you even believe this of her?"

"Her letters to Gladys weren't explicit, but it was clear she was seeking advice for something Gladys had experienced. She was going to Memphis," Hick said.

Wheeler's eyes widened. "What?"

"Susie was planning to go to Memphis. Gladys was going to give her an address, but we don't know if Susie ever got the information."

Dumbfounded, the reverend whispered. "Susie was going to Memphis?"

"We speculate she was going to have the baby in Memphis and put it up for adoption. Everyone knows Gladys knew of an agency."

"Susie was going to Memphis." Wheeler's voice was barely audible.

"If that baby had been Ronnie's," Hick said, "I think Susie would have told him. Everyone expected them to marry anyway. The fact that she was so secretive, that she was so frightened makes me think there was someone else involved, someone she might have felt she needed to protect. If we confirm she was pregnant, it may help us get to the bottom of all of this."

"What?" Wheeler asked his eyes flitting from Adam to Hick.

"If Susie wasn't pregnant, we're back to square one," Hick admitted.

"So you want to dig up my child to satisfy a hunch?" Wheeler shook his head, clearly upset. A resolute gleam came upon his face. "If I sign that paper and she's not pregnant I'm going straight to Murphy, you understand? I'm going to tell him how you men bullied me and threatened my baby's reputation and how shameful this all is. And then I'm going to my lawyer. I will accuse you of slander. Susie can't defend herself from your accusations."

Adam and Hick looked at each other. "It's a chance we're willing to take," Hick said.

Wheeler looked up at Doc Prescott. "And you? Jake, you're a part of this?"

"In this situation," Jake replied, "when there are the lives of two young men at stake—"

"Men." Wheeler snorted and shook his head. "Animals more like." He drew in a deep breath. "Give me the form. I want to hear nothing more of this until you come crawling for forgiveness because of what you've put me through here tonight. Of course, her mother will hear nothing of this until after my lawyer contacts you."

Jake put the affidavit on the desk in front of Reverend Wheeler and he signed it firmly and then glared at them. "Now, gentlemen, if you don't mind, get the hell off my property."

12

The plan was simple enough. Hick took Jake back to his office with instructions to wait for the arrival of the coffin. In the meantime, at 9:45 p.m., Adam would hurry from the station with the squad car's lights and siren blazing. Presumably, Wayne Murphy would follow. If Hick knew Wayne, he would be waiting for just such an occurrence. But if he didn't take the bait, they would be in trouble.

"He'll follow come hell or high water," Adam said with a laugh. "I'll lead him on a wild goose chase he won't soon forget."

"Where you gonna go?"

"I reckon he'll follow me all the way to Pocahontas. Once I get there, I'll just switch off the lights and get a cup of coffee. That'll make him madder than hell and ought to give you plenty of time to get the coffin to Doc's office."

"Seth McDaniel's got the back hoe ready," Hick said. "I'm sure he finds this all a little strange, but I trust him."

To pass the time, Hick lit a cigarette and began looking

through the box they had taken from the school. Susie Wheeler's student file was there and seemed intact. Thumbing through it, Hick saw she was an exceptionally good student and well liked. She had few absences, good grades, and was involved in several after school programs, including the Music club, Pep club, and student council. He held up the picture clipped in her student record, the last photo made of Susie. There was a sweetness in her expression, a child-like innocence. How could someone like Susie end up murdered?

"Hick." Adam's voice said cutting through his musings. "It's time."

"You ready?"

"Yeah. Let's do this." Adam's eyes shone with excitement. "I've been waitin' for a chance to teach that bastard a lesson."

With that, Adam took a deep breath, winked, and rushed from the building, making as much noise as possible. He opened the trunk, for no good reason, and let it fall with a bang. Then, he climbed into the driver's seat, started the car, and turned on the lights and siren. He revved the engine and let the siren wail for a minute, then took off down the road, fast enough to be interesting without being dangerous.

Hick stood back in the shadows and watched through the window. For a moment, he feared their plan hadn't worked because the newspaper office remained dark, quiet. Then the door opened and Wayne Murphy emerged, hobbling out to his car, stamping his shoes on his feet, and buckling his belt. Murphy dropped his car keys and Hick imagined him cussing a blue streak. He climbed in his car, slammed the door, and sped off after Adam. Hick watched the car until it was out of sight and then slipped out the back door of the station and walked to the cemetery.

Seth McDaniel, the undertaker, waited with his two oldest sons. "You sure ol' man Wheeler's okay with this?" Seth was wiry, with dark eyes, sallow skin, and few teeth.

"He don't like it much," Hick said. "But he signed the affidavit to exhume her." Hick produced the affidavit with the angry signature of the Reverend Ted Wheeler. Once the autopsy was complete it would be as if Susie was never exhumed. She would be back in the grave, and Hick would make the affidavit disappear.

"Why can't it wait until morning?"

"Seth, I can't tell you anything yet. Just make it so nobody knows Susie ain't here anymore. Cover this up the best you can. Hopefully, Susie's back at rest before anyone notices she's gone."

Seth spit a stream of tobacco juice onto the grass and screwed his face up. "I don't like it one bit, but I abide by the law."

Seth took the backhoe and began to remove dirt. The smell of soil filled Hick's nostrils and his feet grew cold standing in the wet grass. The damp settled through the seams in his leather shoes and into his socks. Luckily, disinterring the coffin took very little time. The delta soil was so sandy it was harder to keep dirt from washing away than from settling in. Many of the tombstones were sinking at odd angles and several graves appeared as if their inhabitants had tried some sort of escape.

"There it is," Seth told Hick after several more scoops of sandy dirt were removed. Hick watched as Seth's son Ben climbed down into the grave and put two ropes around the coffin. He climbed out and the four men stood silently, peering into the hole where the coffin rested in a muddy pool of water.

Seth McDaniel told Hick, "We're gonna do this respect-ful but quick. You stand up straight and lift hand over hand. You feel your feet start to slip or like you're fixin' to fall, you signal and we stop until you get your footing. We drop the coffin, it's gonna bust and I don't treat my people like that. Got it?"

Hick licked his lips and nodded. The situation was unset-tling and he felt a chill prick at his spine. Grasping the rope, he began lifting. The coffin was heavy and the rope burned his hands. The McDaniels were used to this sort of work, but Hick would have blisters in the morning. He slipped one time and bent over. "Stand up straight," Seth barked. "You'll throw your back out."

After what seemed a very long time, but in reality was only minutes, the coffin was up from the hole. The four men shifted forward, the box dangling from the ropes and sat the casket on the grass in front of the grave. Then, using the handles on the sides, they lifted it into the waiting hearse.

Hick wiped his hands on his pants and shook Seth's hand. "I appreciate you keeping this quiet."

"I don't like it none, but I like I said, I abide by the law. I'll take her to doc's office and leave her there. I'll be back to get her tomorrow at dawn. Won't need you to put her back.

Got a machine for lowering 'em. Ain't all that often we lift 'em up."

Hick nodded and watched as Seth climbed into the hearse and drove away. His sons wordlessly turned and walked away leaving Hick alone in the middle of the graveyard. As he stood there he couldn't decide which would be better, to discover Susie was pregnant or that she was not. Either way, the business had been distasteful, and he was glad to begin the walk home in the moonlight.

He put his hands in his pockets as he walked down the gravel road. The sun had dropped below the horizon and the hum of crickets and toads filled the air. Hick enjoyed the nighttime. In spite of the fact that he never carried a gun, he felt safe and peaceful in the darkness. The darkness quieted his thoughts and stopped them from swirling and tormenting him.

As he neared the house, he was surprised to find Maggie sitting on the porch swing, cradling the baby. She looked rattled, her face was flushed and her eyes were red when Hick got to the porch.

"What's wrong?" he asked alarmed at her appearance.

She forced a smile. "Nothing, Hickory. I just got startled."

Hick was unconvinced. Maggie was not easily frightened. "What startled you?"

She sighed. "I just came outside to watch the last piece of the sunset and to get some air. I heard something and that Delaney boy, the twin, came creepin' around the corner. He purt near scared me to death. I hollered and I reckon I scared him too 'cause he took off running."

Hick felt his stomach tighten. It had been a long day, he had not slept, and he was irritable and on edge. His blood raced through his veins and his heart began to pound. "Get in the house," he ordered through gritted teeth.

"What?" Maggie asked with wide eyes.

"Get in the house! I'm goin' after that little bastard."

"Hickory," Maggie began, but he interrupted her. "That boy's got no call to come skulking around here when I'm not home." He turned and headed toward the car.

"Hickory," Maggie protested. "He didn't do nothing. He just frightened me, that's all."

"Scaring you is enough," he said slowly. "Lock the doors."

With shaking hands Hick guided the key into the ignition, started the car, and sped off down the gravel road. He watched in the rear view mirror as Maggie stood helplessly watching, then she turned and went inside.

Hick's heart thudded in his chest and blood throbbed at his temples. How dare that kid come onto his property and scare his wife? What was wrong with these people? Was the whole tribe murderous? He remembered Job's surly face the day he and Adam visited their shack. What if he had hurt Maggie? What if he had laid a hand on her? His face flushed with anger, his jaw clenched, and his breath was coming in gasps. As he sped along the road a familiar figure came into view in the line of his headlights. He raced the car ahead of the boy and turned sideways into the ditch blocking him. The he jumped out of the car and pounced on Job Delaney, slamming him into the back quarter panel.

Holding him roughly by the shoulders, Hick growled,

"Tell me why I shouldn't beat the hell out of you right here and leave you bloody in the ditch?"

Hick's eyes settled on Job's face, swollen and red, and he realized the boy had been crying. An overwhelming feeling of shame swept over him, and he was filled with horror. Reverend Wheeler's disease had afflicted him as well.

He loosened his hold on Job. "I shouldn't have done that. What's happened, Job?"

The boy ran his sleeve under his nose and sniffed. "It's mama. Doc Prescott's at the house and told me to fetch you." His eyes welled. "She's dyin'. Doc says she wants to talk to you."

"To me?" Hick asked in some surprise.

The boy nodded.

"Get in the car. We'll go together."

Job rubbed his shoulders as he climbed in the car which only made Hick more disgusted with himself. He gripped the steering wheel and turned to look at the boy. "Job, I'm sorry about that." The boy didn't turn, didn't say a word, just continued to peer out the window. An occasional sniff was the only sound he made.

The coal oil lantern was burning in the front room as Hick and Job arrived. Mourning was crying and when she saw her twin she rushed across the room and clung to his neck. Doc Prescott turned and shook his head. Pearl Delaney was dead.

Her two children were crying softly in the corner. "Do you know what she wanted to see me about?" Hick asked the doctor in a quiet voice.

"She told me she needed to tell you something about Susie Wheeler."

"Susie Wheeler?"

"She wouldn't tell me what it was. Said she could only talk to you." Doc shook his head sadly. "Pearl maintained Abner's innocence until her death. I reckon her last thoughts on earth were about her boys and their safety."

"I can understand that," Hick replied remembering his own quickness to judge Job Delaney.

The doctor indicated the twins. "What do we do about those two? They can't stay out here alone."

At thirteen, Job and Mourning Delaney were too young to care for themselves. Hick turned to them. "Ya'll got kin that can look after you?"

Mourning shook her head. "No, Sheriff. Our kin disowned us when Daddy went to the pen. We ain't seen hide nor hair of none of 'em in years."

As Hick looked at the children he thought of his encounter with Job and saw the shock and terror in the boy's eyes. Unlike most of Cherokee Crossing, he didn't believe the Delaneys were trouble and yet, even he had rushed to judgment. As he thought all this over he made an uncharacteristic, impulsive decision. "Get what you need. You're coming with me."

Job and Mourning stared wide-eyed at Hick and turned to each other. Then they went to the back of the house to gather what little clothing they owned.

Jake Prescott looked surprised. "You think Maggie will be alright with that?" he asked after they left the room.

Hick nodded. "You know Mag and kids. If I don't bring 'em back with me, I'll get an earful."

"But with the baby ..." Jake questioned.

"Doc, I gotta help her more. I know I gotta help her more. These two will only be with us until Eben and Jed get back. Eben's seventeen so I reckon he can care for 'em." He indicated the wasted state of Pearl Delaney. "He's been carin' for 'em for years."

The doctor nodded and Job and Mourning came out of the back room each with an armful of old clothes. "You takin' us to jail?" Mourning asked wide-eyed.

"I'm takin' you to my house," Hick replied.

"Your woman ain't gonna want us there," Job said cautiously.

"My 'woman' will be fine with it. You just scared her earlier, that's all."

The twins looked at one another. "But what about mama?" Mourning asked tears beginning to puddle in her eyes. "What will happen to mama?"

The doctor patted her shoulder. "Mourning, I got some money set aside. I'll bury her for you."

Now it was Hick's turn to be surprised. The doctor just shrugged. "Pearl Delaney has been my 'colleague' in this town for decades. There was more to her potions than most people would have guessed." He looked at the wasted face on the pillow. "She had my respect."

Mourning dropped her clothes and ran to the bed, clinging to her mother. The doctor helped her up and together he and Hick put the Delaneys into the car.

In spite of a warm welcome from Maggie and a clean, comfortable bed, when Hick woke before dawn the next morning, the children were already gone.

13

Maggie paced the kitchen floor and fretted over Jimmy, but Hick knew what was wrong.

"They'll be okay, Mag." He sipped his coffee and stared unhappily out the window. "I wish they hadn't gone," he admitted, "but those kids know how to survive."

"But they're just children."

Hick put the coffee cup down and rose from the table. He put his hand on his wife's shoulder and she reached up and grabbed it, her worried eyes met his.

"I have to meet Doc at his office this morning. As soon as I'm done, I'll go back out to their house and see if they went home. If they did, I'll try and talk 'em into coming back. But I can't make 'em stay here."

"You will try?" Maggie asked.

"I'll do my best. Those kids have never had a chance. I'd like to help 'em if I can."

She leaned into him, looking up into his eyes. "I knew you would."

He bent to give her and Jimmy a kiss and picked up his hat. "I'll try to be home for dinner."

She nodded and he walked out of the house, pausing on the porch to listen to the sounds of the fading night. He climbed into the car, not anxious to hear what Jake Prescott had to say and even less anxious to see what remained of Susie Wheeler after fourteen years in the grave.

It was dark and Hick's headlights cast weird shadows on the shrubs near Jake's porch as he pulled up to the office. He knew the doctor would be in the back so he went around the corner of the white clapboard house that served as both residence and office and knocked on the screen door.

"Hick?" Jake called.

"Yeah."

"Come on in."

Hick tentatively walked into the office and was relieved to see the coffin lid had already been replaced. Jake was in his white lab coat and was putting instruments away.

"Well?" Hick asked.

Jake nodded. "You and Adam guessed right." He went over to a small table on wheels and picked up a metal tray. On it lay an assortment of what looked like chicken bones. Taking his cigar from his mouth he pointed with it saying, "These were found in the pelvic area. Susie Wheeler appears to have been about four months pregnant when she died."

Hick stared at the dish, an overwhelming sadness welling up inside.

"Where does the case go from here?" Jake asked.

"Someone out there had motive to kill Susie Wheeler. I

think Gladys figured out who that was and that's what got her killed. Now, I need to figure out who it was."

"I see," Jake answered.

Hick sat down and let his mind race. Susie Wheeler was pregnant and Gladys provided her with an address for an adoption agency. But who else knew Susie was pregnant? How did they know Susie would be out by the slough at that time of day? Was she meeting the baby's father? Hick looked up at Jake. "I need to find out more about Susie's last days … who she was with, who might have known her troubles. I need to talk to Wheeler."

"I'll go with you," the doctor volunteered.

Hick turned away as Jake lifted the lid to Susie's coffin and returned the bones of her child to their rightful place. Then, they waited until after Seth McDaniel had retrieved Susie's casket to call on the Reverend and Mrs. Wheeler. The sun had risen and the day promised to be clear as the squad car pulled into the large circular drive in front of the home. Hick paused and closed his eyes. "This won't go well."

"I know," Jake agreed. "Let's just get it over with."

Nodding, Hick opened the door of his car and was dumbfounded to hear the crack of a rifle ring out from behind the house.

"What the hell?" he shouted and then ran around the corner of the house leaving Jake trudging behind.

He reached the back yard to be greeted by a triumphant Ted Wheeler. The rifle in his hand still smoked.

"I got him!" he yelled at Hick. "I got the beast. He would

have killed us." He was giddy and began to laugh. "I did it! I did it!"

His shouts and laughter were halted by an inhuman sounding wail coming from the back of his property. Jake arrived at that moment and ran toward the source of the sound. Racing through the yard, Hick stopped short, horrified at what he saw. Mourning Delaney was bent over her dying twin, screaming and crying, ripping the hair from her head in clumps.

Wheeler caught up, breathing heavily from the run and then froze, as if seeing a nightmare unfold before him. Mourning never looked up, her eyes were filled with the form of her brother, bleeding profusely from a wound in his back. In Job's hands were the remains of the Reverend Wheeler's breakfast, crusts of toast, burnt bacon, and apple cores. Hick suddenly realized the dark, shadowy figure that was spreading panic throughout the town of Cherokee Crossing was nothing more than Job Delaney trying to put food on the table for his mother and sister by any means possible ... even if that meant rifling through the diner garbage.

Jake bent down and felt Job's wrist, then shook his head. Placing his hands on Mourning's shoulders he said, "Come, child. Come with me."

"Noooo," she screamed and pulled away. Their limbs had intertwined in the womb, their hearts had beat in unison since the moment they were conceived and now Mourning Delaney, for the first time in her existence, was alone.

Jake tried to pull her away, but she fought back frantically, grasping her brother's waist, his blood covering her arms and chest.

"Mourning, he's gone," Hick said quietly, kneeling beside her and placing his hand on her head.

She howled and pressed her face against Job's bloodied shirt.

"Mourning …"

She screamed once more, a desperate, heartbroken wail that caused the hair on Hick's arms to stand up, and then she collapsed into sobs, still clinging to her dead twin.

Hick turned to Wheeler who stood there aghast, mouth hanging open, a look of shock and horror on his face. "I thought he was Jed … or Eben. I thought he was…."

"He was what?" Hick stood and faced the reverend, rage coursing through him. "Coming to hurt you? Or your wife? For what purpose? To what end? Why would they have anything against you? What reason would they have to come here and start trouble?"

"Reason?" the minister asked, as if he didn't understand the word.

"Reason. The thing that should set us apart from animals. The common sense that God gives us, but people like you throw out the minute you feel threatened. You called Abner Delaney an animal. What are you? The minute you feel threatened, your only thought is self-preservation. You'll do anything to survive. Chew your leg off. Kill an innocent child. Anything! Like a fox, caught in a trap."

The rifle dropped from Ted Wheeler's hand as Jake helped

the still sobbing Mourning to her feet. Her brother's blood covered her, matted in her hair and smeared across her face. As Jake led her to Hick's car, Hick turned to the reverend and said in a flat voice, "By the way, we came out here to tell you Susie was about four month's pregnant when she died."

Ted Wheeler aged before Hick's eyes. His frame sagged as if gravity had suddenly grabbed hold, pressing him down toward the earth. "What?" His voice was barely audible.

"I'm going to need to ask you and your wife a few questions. Right now, I'm taking Mourning Delaney to my house. The undertaker will be out here for Job. Don't touch anything and wait inside. There will probably be charges." Hick pulled his handkerchief from his pocket and lifted the warm rifle from the earth.

Ted Wheeler nodded, his eyes fastened to the remains of the boy.

Hick sighed. "I understand fear is a powerful thing to control. I was in Europe, I've done plenty of things to be ashamed of. But you … you brought this on yourself. You could have been teaching love and tolerance and understanding. You could have been asking your congregation to have patience and let us do our job. Instead, you chose to spread hate and fear. Hate is an all-consuming thing. It always destroys."

"I didn't mean to kill—" Wheeler began, but he couldn't finish. Sobs erupted from somewhere deep within him.

The reverend stood sobbing in the yard as Hick walked away. The blood of Job Delaney seeped into the ground.

Hick marched around the house toward the squad car,

the rifle in his hand as heavy and burdensome as anything he had ever carried.

Mrs. Wheeler stood on the porch, wringing her hands, and looking at the back seat of the car where Jake sat wiping the blood from Mourning's face. "What's happened, Sheriff?"

"Your husband has been involved in an altercation," he told her as he opened the trunk and placed the rifle inside. "I'm gonna need you to call the station and have Wash or Adam come out."

"An altercation?"

"He killed a trespasser," Hick said, slamming the trunk with vehemence he couldn't control.

She staggered backward and sank down into a wicker chair. "Killed?"

"Yes, a young boy. Job Delaney."

"Delaney?"

"Yes, ma'am. He was in your fire barrel, looking for breakfast."

She stared at the car where the still-frantic Mourning was clearly visible

"Breakfast ..." Her voice trailed off. "Will he ... will he go to prison?"

Hick followed her gaze back to the car. "Men like him don't go to prison."

14

Ted Wheeler had aged ten years by the time Hick returned to the house. The Reverend's face was haggard and drawn, the smug, haughty look gone. His hands trembled and he sat in a chair staring out the window. Hick joined Wash in the front room and Mrs. Wheeler handed him a cup of coffee, sat the pot on the coffee table in the front room, and retreated to a wingback chair where her knitting lay nearby. Wash stood in the doorway, cup in hand, watching Wheeler. A gentle breeze wafted the white curtains at the windows, ushering in the scents of grass and lilac.

Hick took a sip of coffee and looked at Wheeler. "You want to tell us what happened?"

The reverend jumped at the sound of Hick's voice. "Happened?"

Hick drew in a breath, struggling to control his temper. In truth he was so goddamned angry, he cared not a whit about sparing Wheeler's feelings, but he needed information and knew the best way to get it was to remain calm.

"Tell me why you shot Job."

"It was the dog," Wheeler answered in a shaky voice. "I was over there in my study, and I heard the dog barking." He removed his glasses to clean them but stopped. "I thought maybe it was one of his brothers, up to no good. They've been all over town causing trouble."

"Have they?" Hick asked in a low, bitter voice.

"They've been sneaking around and—"

Hick interrupted. "I just had word from the state troopers in Illinois. They traced them up there and are checking the strawberry patches. We know they were at Litchfield because Buckley at the bank said they sent in a cash deposit after they finished picking."

Wheeler looked up. "They're not even here?"

"No, they haven't been here for four days. I guess putting food on the table seemed to be more important than molesting all you upstanding citizens."

The glasses slid onto the floor. "But—"

"What happened after you heard the dog barking?" Wash prompted with no emotion. At sixty-three years old, Deputy Wash Metcalfe was little help when it came to leg work, but Hick was always impressed with his passionless, yet effective questioning. Hick knew Wash realized he had made a mistake fourteen years ago. He would not be making the same mistake again.

Wheeler's eyes went from Hick to Wash and he ran his hand over his forehead. "I don't … I heard the dog, and I got up from my desk to see what he was barking at. I spied someone at the back of the yard by the trash barrel."

"Where was the rifle?" Wash asked.

"In an upstairs closet."

"So you saw a person in the yard and went to get your rifle?" Wash offered.

"Yes."

"Was the figure in the yard behaving suspiciously?" Wash moved forward and sat the coffee cup down.

"No, but he was in my yard—"

"Did you feel threatened at any time?"

"Well, no, not exactly." Wheeler responded, his face tight with agitation.

"Did it occur to you at any time that it might be a neighbor, or someone from town taking a walk, just wandering through, looking for something?"

Wheeler shook his head.

"So," Hick said, taking up the questioning, "You heard the dog barking and immediately went upstairs to get a weapon?"

"Everyone had been saying—"

"Saying what?" Hick's voice rose with frustration. "That the Delaney brothers were on some sort of murderous rampage? That after all these years of hard work and toil, they were out to spill innocent blood? For what? The fun of it?"

Wheeler looked at his hands and made no answer. Hick shook his head. He could barely stand to look at the man. "I warned you, Wheeler. I told you that if you didn't stop filling everyone's heads with hate, no good would come of it."

Ted Wheeler's haunted eyes rested on Hick's face. "How is the little girl?" he asked in a broken voice.

"Hopefully sleeping. Doc gave her something and he and my wife are taking care of her."

"I didn't know ..." Wheeler said, his voice cracking and his eyes trailing to the window.

"You worked yourself up into a lather. You worked half the town up into a lather. What did you think would happen?"

The reverend sat unmoving in the chair near the window as if wishing himself to another place and time. In the hour that had passed since Job Delaney was shot Reverend Wheeler seemed to shrink into himself. He'd been diminished, while his wife's presence expanded to fill the space left behind. "What happens now?" she asked from the corner of the room.

"We'll charge your husband with manslaughter; the district attorney will look at the case. They'll note that the boy was trespassing on your property. They'll also note that Job Delaney was poor, uneducated, the son of a convicted murderer, and that you are upstanding members of the community." Hick shrugged. "In all probability, nothing will happen."

Reverend Wheeler's eyes widened. "But he's dead."

"Welcome to the world of 'justice'."

Mrs. Wheeler could not hide the obvious relief from her face. As much as he wanted to, Hick couldn't begrudge her audible exhalation of relief. And yet, there was a sadness that lingered. "My little Susie ... tell me, Sheriff. What does the fact that she was ... what does any of this mean?"

"You had no inkling your daughter was pregnant?" Hick took a seat on the couch opposite Mrs. Wheeler.

She shook her head. "Not until Ted told me today. She was a good girl. I can't imagine how it happened."

"Can you tell me anything about Susie's final months? Who were her friends? Where she spent her time?"

"But, why?" Mrs. Wheeler asked in a tear-filled voice. "What does Susie have to do with any of this?"

"Because I don't believe Gladys Kestrel was the only person to know Susie was pregnant. There were two parties involved … there always are. I believe Abner Delaney was simply at the wrong place, at the wrong time. Like Eben and Jed … and Job."

The Reverend Wheeler looked up. "But he was—"

"Executed?" Hick finished the sentence and rubbed his hand roughly across his mouth in frustration. "I can't prove it yet, but I believe Abner Delaney was executed for a crime he did not commit. I believe he was innocent, and I intend to prove it."

Ted Wheeler's face crumbled. His mouth twitched and his nostrils flared. "I have hated Abner Delaney with all the energy of my being for over a decade." He seemed lost, as if he no longer knew what to live for.

Hick studied the reverend. It was clear he was in shock and would be little help. He turned his attention back to Mrs. Wheeler. "Do you know why Susie was out by the slough that day? Did she frequently walk there?"

"No. I never knew Susie to go there. She just didn't come home from school that day." Mrs. Wheeler's eyes filled with tears. "We didn't get to say good-bye." She wiped them quickly and continued. "Susie was seeing Ronnie Pringle at the time she was killed. But I don't know when they would have had the opportunity to … Ted made sure they did their courtin' here. In the front room."

"Even if Ronnie were still alive, I wouldn't take the time to talk to him. Had he been the father, he would have made it right and married Susie. That I don't doubt for a minute. The fact that Susie confided in Gladys Kestrel tells me she never told Ronnie. It's pretty hard to convince a man he's the father of your child when you haven't had relations." Hick shifted uneasily on the hard couch. "No, it's pretty clear Susie didn't want you or Ronnie to know she was pregnant. Were there any other boys Susie was interested in? Any one else she saw?"

"No, Sheriff. Susie was either at school or at home. She didn't spend a lot of time at friends' homes and she didn't go to town on Saturday nights and drive around like so many of the girls. She was quiet. She studied hard and worked hard. I don't understand…"

"What about Gladys? Did you know she and Susie were writing?"

"No. I had no idea Susie ever confided in Gladys."

"So Susie went to school, came straight home and studied every night, is that it?"

"Well, she stayed after school most days because of her activities."

Hick made a note in his book to check her school records and the yearbooks to find out who was with Susie in her after-school clubs. It was clear Ronnie Pringle was not the only boy in Susie's life. Who else did she spend time with?

Hick rose and closed his leather book. "I see no reason to run you in," he told Wheeler. "You're not a flight risk. I'll turn your case over to the District Attorney and you'll hear from him. Deputy Metcalfe here will do the formalities."

The phone rang and Mrs. Wheeler excused herself to answer it.

"And that's it?" Wheeler asked, astounded. He looked up at Hick. In one hour Ted Wheeler had gone from a vindictive hate-monger to this broken shell of a human being and Hick couldn't help but feel it was the reverend's own doing.

"Yeah, that's it." Hick was unable to conceal the bitterness in his voice. He turned to leave, but Mrs. Wheeler stopped him.

"Sheriff, that was Deputy Kinion. There's been a fire at your mother's. She's okay, but you need to head over there now."

A fire? Hick stood, immobilized for a moment and then turned to Wash. "You got everything under control here?"

Wash nodded. "You best get over there."

∾

Pam Kinion was sitting on the porch swing patting her mother's hand when Hick arrived. The smell of smoke was thick.

Hick climbed the steps, and said, "What happened?"

"I don't know." His mother looked from her daughter to her son. "I was frying bacon and I went to get something …"

"How long was it frying?"

"I don't remember."

"I was coming over to see if Mom needed anything from the store," Pam said. "As soon as I got out of the car, I could smell the smoke. I got Mom out and doused it with salt. Adam says we caught it just in time."

Hick's heart pounded at the thought of what might have happened and his palms began to sweat. He knelt in front of his mother, looked into her eyes.

She smiled weakly. "I'm okay. Don't worry yourselves."

He kissed her cheek and went into the house, stopping short just inside the doorway. The smell of smoke clawed at his throat A farmhouse in Belgium filled his field of vision and snow fell around him, melting on his skin. Flames hissed with every flake and the acrid smell of burning gasoline, fabric, and human flesh filled his nostrils. His heart pounded in his ears and his vision swam. He pressed a hand against the door jamb to steady himself.

"The oil got hot enough to ignite," Adam said in a voice that sounded oceans away.

Hick swallowed hard and forced himself to nod, to shut away those memories one more time. He let go of the door jamb and followed Adam into the kitchen. The damage was shocking. The bacon had cooked into leather and flames had exploded up the wall and to the ceiling. Ash and salt lay like a blanket of heavy snow on the stove and the room was filled with greasy, black smoke.

Adam's face was grim. "Much longer and the curtains would have caught and then the roof." He shook his head. "Your mama was very lucky today."

The damage was confined to the corner of the kitchen with the stove. Had Pam not decided to stop by, the outcome would have been completely different. Hick's knees threatened to buckle. He lit a cigarette and shook his head. "How could she have forgotten she was frying bacon?"

Adam closed his eyes and scratched his head. "I don't know, but she's getting worse."

"Jesus," Hick said. Pam and Maggie had been right.

Pam came to the doorway and said, "I'm takin' Mom home with me. She's a little shaken up, and I don't think she should be alone."

Adam nodded. "That sounds like a good idea."

His mother appeared behind Pam. "Oh dear," she said. "What a mess. What am I going to do?"

"Don't worry about it, Ma," Hick told her. "We'll take care of this. You go on with Pam."

"But—"

"Come on Mama," Pam said in a gentle voice. "Let's go on to my house."

She hesitated, appeared uncertain.

"I'll stick around here," Hick said. "I need to go through the study and look through Dad's things anyway." He crossed the kitchen and kissed his mother's forehead. "You go on with Pam and get some rest. I'll keep an eye on the place."

His mother's face lit up with obvious relief. "That would be a comfort to me." He watched Pam help their mother into the car. When had his mother shrunk? She looked so small.

As the car pulled out of the driveway, Hick and Adam went around the house opening windows to let out the choking smoke. In the study, Hick surveyed the papers spread on the desk and shook his head. "We can deal with the kitchen later. We have to find out what on earth Gladys was looking for."

"I'll leave this to you to try to find out," Adam said, turning to go. "Someone needs to get back to the station."

"When you get there, look through those old yearbooks we brought from Gladys' room. After talking with the Wheelers, it seems Ronnie Pringle toed the line. He could be her baby's father, but for some reason it doesn't feel right. See if you can turn someone else up. Someone that was in the same after-school clubs maybe."

"Okay. I'll call you if anything jumps out at me."

The front door closed behind Adam, leaving the house eerily still. Hick crushed out his cigarette in an ashtray and looked about the room. He recalled the patient, wise face of his father, one of the few men on earth who was able to retain his respect. Their last conversation came back to him with all its bitter sweetness. Hick was headed to war and his father knew the boy in Hick would be a casualty. James Blackburn understood, what so many did not, that not all war wounds are visible.

"Hickory, I'd give anything to keep you home with me," he'd said. Hick knew his parents wanted him to go to college and get a deferment. Matt Pringle and some of the other wealthier boys in town had gone that route. But even if Hick wanted to, his grades would not have gotten him into college. He'd had other things on his mind when he'd been in high school. And there was a part of him that wanted to go into the army ... wanted to see the world and to experience the manly art of war. Hick closed his eyes, remembering how stupidly naïve he'd been.

This was his father's domain and Hick felt like an intruder. He lowered himself into his father's chair and began going through the papers on the desk one by one, but there was nothing of note. Tax receipts. Bills from various utilities and handymen. Notes from Jake Prescott detailing the treatment his father had put off until it was too late. Hick stacked these items and placed them back in the right hand drawer.

He opened the drawer on the left and noted it was full of correspondence. He pulled the letters from the drawer. They went back decades. Some were from relatives, long dead. James Blackburn had been the youngest son in a family of seven and the only one who had lived long enough to have children of his own. His longevity in a family of short-lived men only added to the mythology that seemed to follow and haunt him, the notion that he was magical because he was the seventh son of a seventh son. His father had never escaped this idea, at least not with the more superstitious folk in Cherokee Crossing.

He sorted through the letters, mainly from old college friends and colleagues in the vicinity, other principals from nearby school districts. Hick held one up. What exactly was he looking for? The room darkened suddenly and a low rumble of thunder rattled the window panes. Another storm. Seemed like spring had been one storm after another. He glanced out the window and saw billowing clouds moving across a darkening sky. Damn, this one was coming up fast.

He stood and went back around the house closing windows and returned to the study. Flipping on the light, he sat back at his father's desk. A pop of lightning was followed by a long, low growl of thunder and Hick absently noted the wind was picking up. He put aside the letters from old college buddies and family. These did not seem like they would be of any interest to Gladys and he concentrated on the letters from colleagues, thumbing through them to see if anything could be relevant. *Dear Jim*, the first letter read, *You must think of yourself and the family. Even if you take some time off, the school will be there when you return.*

There were many others in that same vein. The principal from Marmaduke telling him, *This isn't something that will take care of itself* and one from Missouri saying, *Your family needs you more than the school. Think of them.*

Hick recalled the willing role he had played in the sham his parents created. He remembered the tales of "sunspots" and "age spots" and how he had believed the lies his parents told him because he wanted to believe them. They never sat down with him and told him his father had cancer. Everything was designed to give him as little as possible to worry about. They could not have known his father would die when Hick was in Europe and that his first letter from home would be the announcement.

An electric blue flash lit up the outside. An ear-shattering crash of thunder followed, and the house went dark. The room seemed to hold its breath, abnormally still and calm even though rain fell in silvery sheets, blowing sideways from the force of the wind that caused the cotton plants across the road to sway and dance wildly. Hick headed to the kitchen to get a candle.

Glancing at the blackened wall, he opened the ice box to see if there was anything there. Shaking his head, he wondered if his mother ever ate. His father would have wanted him to take better care of her. He had let him down again.

He found the white utility candles in a bottom drawer and grabbed a couple and then pulled down the candlesticks. Snatching the last apple in the otherwise-empty fruit bowl, he headed back to the study.

Noon in Arkansas and dark as pitch. Hopefully there wouldn't be a tornado. He lit the candles and ignored the odd shadows flickering on the study's walls. Taking a big bite of the apple, he started in on the letters again.

Many discussed the depression and its effect on the students. Others questioned closing school for October as was the custom in the cotton belt. As Hick read through them, the murder of Gladys Kestrel drifted back further into his mind and was replaced by a swelling pride. So many people had come to his father for advice. Arkansas had long been recognized as lagging in education, and his father had worked hard to change things. He rallied against the notion that high school should be reserved for the privileged few and had increased attendance two-fold during his tenure as principal. He was respected in his community and by his peers.

Despite everything going on around him, Hick was filled with a sense of connection and contentment as he read letter after letter, as if he was sitting with the father he had loved and admired and missed so terribly. And then the warm feeling evaporated and his blood chilled. He sat up straight in his chair and re-read the letter in his hand. The candles flickered wildly as his breath quickened. Then the letter fell to the desktop and he covered his face with his hands.

15

The driving rain pounded on the windshield, the wipers barely able to keep up. Hick's mind raced, and he gripped the steering wheel, not even trying to stay within the speed limit. His back tires hydroplaned as he took a corner too fast. He righted the car and sped toward the station, throwing open the door and running inside, not caring about the rain blowing into his face. Rain dripped from the brim of his hat as he hung it on the rack and he wiped it from his forehead with a sleeve. Wordlessly, he crossed the room.

"What's going on?" Adam asked, looking up from the stack of yearbooks he was inspecting.

Hick flung the lid off the box marked 1936 that they'd brought back from the school. Frantically he searched through the folders and then looked at Adam. "It's not here."

"What?"

"George Shelley's personnel record. It's missing."

"Maybe it was sent to Pocahontas when he transferred."

"No," Hick said. "There would have been a copy, at least of what he'd done at Cherokee Crossing. He was here for half the year."

"What are you saying?" Adam asked, rising from his desk and walking toward Hick.

Hick handed him the letter. "What does this mean to you?"

Adam read the letter out loud and his face grew ashen.

"I am taking Mr. Shelley as an employee, but only as a personal favor to you, Jim. You must understand, he will not be permitted to interact with any of the students on an extra-curricular basis. He must be made aware of the fact that I know your suspicions about what might have occurred there in Cherokee Crossing with the young lady and that I will not tolerate any hint of that within my schools. I agree to your request to not put any of this in his permanent record, however, if anything occurs here, in this school system, it will be duly noted."

Adam put the letter down and crossed the room with Hick on his heels. The yearbooks were open on Adam's desk.

"I was looking for a student, not a faculty member," he said. He pulled out a pen and circled the smiling face of George Shelley as he posed with the student council, with the music club, and with the pep club. Beside him in every picture stood a young, beautiful Susie Wheeler. Adam frowned. "Shit. It's never easy, is it?"

"No," Hick replied. "You think Shelley's our man? You think he killed Gladys … and Susie for that matter?"

"He certainly had motive. And if someone took his personnel record that means they thought there might be something that needed to be hidden."

"And my dad knew along …" His stomach was queasy and a sour taste erupted at the back of his throat.

Adam shook his head. "I don't think so. I think he suspected and his suspicions were enough for him to want to separate George and Susie and to ask Principal Knowles at Pocahontas to take him."

"No." Hick pointed at Shelley's picture. "There had to be more than suspicion for my dad to take a man and his wife and uproot their family from a community they were just becoming a part of. George wouldn't have gone so easily if—"

"But Pocahontas was such a great opportunity."

"So we thought when he left. But if you read the letter you see he actually took a pay cut and a lesser position. He went from high school to grade school and he was forbidden to take part in after school activities. Dad told the Pocahontas principal enough to make him not trust George around students. What George did was wrong. Dad should have exposed him for what he was rather than just send him away."

"Exposed him as what? Your dad didn't know Susie was pregnant or that anything had actually happened. Remember, the letter says 'suspicions' not allegations."

"My dad always thought the best of everyone. For him to even have a hunch that something like that was taking place … no, he had to have had a pretty good idea. In his wildest imaginations, he would never dream up something like George sleeping with Susie unless there was a reason."

"Which is why I don't think he believed anything really happened," Adam countered as he glanced through the yearbook once more.

"It was his job to protect his students—" Hick rubbed his chin and started pacing.

"Which is exactly what he thought he was doing."

"But what about the students at the other school? Didn't he care anything about them? He was putting them in danger."

"Your dad passed his suspicions on to the other principal and the fact that George was never in trouble, that there was never as much as a whisper about him doing anything wrong at Pocahontas, and that he was eventually promoted to vice-principal of the high school … doesn't that justify what your dad did?"

"There weren't any whispers here either, and yet we have a dead girl who was four months pregnant and a dead secretary. Jesus Christ, Adam, Susie was only seventeen."

"Hick, George Shelley was closer in age to Susie Wheeler than I am to Pam."

"True, but he had a wife. How could my dad not see how wrong it was? How could he just pass him to another school and let him get away with it? Did he wonder when Susie died if George killed her or did he assume like everyone else that Abner snapped and killed her for no reason?"

Adam pointed at a picture of Ronnie Pringle and Susie

Wheeler at a class barbecue. "What about Ronnie? What if he found out about George and Susie? Jealousy is a strong motive."

"I'd buy that, but Ronnie's dead so how would Gladys fit in?" Hick sighed and ran his fingers through his hair. "Hell, maybe she doesn't fit in at all. Maybe we're just barkin' up the wrong tree with all of this."

"I don't know," Adam said. "But we've got to go talk to George, find out what he knew about Susie … about her pregnancy. We need to see him."

"Yes, we need to see him. But damn, why does it always have to be so hard?"

∾

"Your mama's house just burned, Hickory. What's so important that you need to leave now?" Maggie stood with her hands on her hips, obviously frustrated that Hick was, once again, heading out of town.

"She's with Pam and the house will be fine."

"I know, but she thinks you're staying there."

"What do you want me to do?" There was a sharp edge to Hick's voice that he regretted immediately.

"What's wrong?"

"Nothing,"

"Nothing?" She picked up Hick's thermos and poured coffee into for the third time this week.

"Maybe I'm just tired from all this traveling."

"I'm glad you're taking Adam this time. Let him drive."

"Yeah," Hick agreed. He glanced out the kitchen window to see Mourning Delaney rocking the baby on the porch swing. He hadn't realized he was staring until he felt Maggie's fingers cup his chin, directing his gaze toward her.

"Hickory, what's happened?"

He recognized the tightness in her voice. The sound that crept up when she was trying to get him to speak, to tell her something, anything, and the weariness and exhaustion of it all was too much.

"Just something I found at work."

Her fingers dug a little into his chin and her gaze held his relentlessly. "What did you find?"

"A letter." His eyes trailed away.

"A letter?"

He nodded and moved away from her grabbing boot covers for his shoes in case it rained.

Maggie crossed the room and closed the front door so Mourning couldn't hear. "Hickory?" She sat at the table and patted the chair beside her. "Talk to me."

He sighed and sat across from her putting his elbows on the table wearily. "I found a letter from Jerry Knowles, the old principal at Pocahontas."

"And?"

"He was talking about George Shelley."

"George Shelley? What about him?"

"Apparently my dad thought George was having an inappropriate relationship with one of the students. That's why he transferred mid-year."

Maggie knit her brow in thought. "Pam said all the girls

were in love with him. He was young and good looking. They called him Professor Dreamboat."

"Yeah?" Hick answered, his voice rising slightly. "Well, apparently 'Professor Dreamboat' and Susie Wheeler were a bit of an item."

Maggie's eyes widened. "Susie Wheeler? You're kidding."

"I wish I was."

"I still don't understand …" Maggie sat back in the chair as if she'd been struck. "Poor Elizabeth," she breathed.

Hick traced a pattern on the kitchen table with his finger and said, "I'm hoping I never have to tell her. There's no point in telling her anything at all." He closed his eyes. "Unless … I hope to God we're wrong … about all of it." He looked into her face. "You know, my dad probably knew all about Susie and George and never did anything about it. Adultery with a student and he just passed George along, reputation intact. And Susie died and I have to wonder if all this is connected with Gladys."

"What?" Maggie's mouth opened and her face whitened. "Hickory, what are you saying? You don't think George …"

"I don't know, Mag, but Adam and I need to talk to George. George is apparently not the man I thought he was and neither was my dad."

"Oh, Hickory," Maggie said, her voice soft, comforting. "Don't do this. Don't do this to yourself or to your dad."

"What am I supposed to think?"

"Don't think anything, until you know the truth. You don't know what happened, what George told your dad. Get all of your facts before you make a judgment. You've always

done that before, and I love that about you. You never jump
to conclusions. You didn't jump to conclusions about Jed
and Eben Delaney. Give your dad the same benefit of the
doubt."

Hick exhaled loudly and nodded his head. "You're right."
He rose from the table and bent to kiss Maggie's forehead.
"I need to get going."

"Thank you," she said, standing and wrapping her arms
around his neck.

"For what?" He asked, breathing in her smell. The same
perfume she'd always worn, but now mingled with the scent
of motherhood.

"Thank you for telling me. For talking to me."

He pulled her close, kissed her hair. "Are you going to be
okay here alone with Mourning?"

"We'll be fine. I think being around Jimmy helps to
take her mind off … off everything."

"Okay. I should be back by bedtime."

He kissed her, one long good-bye kiss and headed out the
door to meet Adam for the long drive to Tennessee.

∾

It was close to four o'clock when George Shelley greeted
Hick and Adam with a surprised smile after answering their
knock on the schoolhouse door. "Hickory Blackburn and
Adam Kinion, what a surprise." They all shook hands and
he ushered them in. "Come in. Come in."

Turning, he walked into the school saying, "Liz just

made a huge batch of her famous chicken salad. She'll give it to me good if I don't bring you boys home for some of it. What do you say?"

"George, this isn't a social call." Adam's voice was low, firm.

George's brow lifted. "Oh?"

Hick glanced at the janitorial staff waxing the wooden floors. "Can we speak somewhere in private?"

"Of course." George led them into his office and closed the door. He motioned to a couple of chairs and leaned against his desk. "What can I do for you?"

Hick hesitated. "We need to ask you some questions of a delicate nature." George nodded and Hick continued. "It has to do with Susie Wheeler."

The color drained from George's face and his mouth crimped into a thin line. "I see." His voice was barely audible.

"When did you find out she was pregnant?" Adam said.

George's knees buckled and he grasped the edge of his desk. "What?"

"We need to know when you learned she was going to have a baby … your baby." Hick watched George's expressions, his every movement, the intake of every breath.

"My baby?" he repeated and raised a trembling hand to his face. He stared down at his shoes and said nothing for a long while. Finally, he looked up. "I'm sorry. I didn't know."

"Why don't you sit down," Hick suggested. "You need to tell us the whole story."

George obediently sat and then looked up at Hick. "Why was there no mention of a baby before now?"

"Information has come to light," Hick said carefully. "But we need you to tell us everything that happened between you and Susie. Everything."

"But why bring this up ... now?"

"We need answers, George," Adam said. "How long were you and Susie Wheeler involved sexually?"

George stared at Adam a moment as if waking from a nightmare. "Not long," he replied. "It started out innocently enough. These things always do. We were together three or four days a week. She always stayed longer than the other kids at the after school functions. Wasn't in a hurry to get home to that dictator of a father, you know." He rose from his chair and looked out the window with his back to Hick and Adam. "She confided in me. She was lonely. Her parents didn't give her much leeway. She didn't have many friends. It's hard to be a teenage girl that is expected to stay at home every night knowing the other girls are out having a good time. I wanted to help her. To give her someone to talk to. I felt sorry for her."

He sighed. "Strangely enough I started confiding in her. Liz hated Cherokee Crossing at first, and she hated me for taking her there. We went days without speaking." He laughed bitterly. "Susie would tell me a woman should support her husband. But Liz ..." He shook his head and turned to face Hick and Adam. "Susie and I were two unhappy people who found a little happiness in each other. Is that such a bad thing?"

"Bad enough to get you transferred and demoted. What were you thinking, George? She was a student and you were a married man." Hick shook his head and swallowed hard. He hesitated before asking, "How much of this did my dad know?"

"Enough to get me moved, but not enough to get me fired." George ran his hands through his hair. "He never had proof, but he noticed Susie stayed around after everyone else went home. He noticed we were together more than he thought was normal for a student-teacher relationship. When he transferred me he told me it was for my own good. He said I was in danger of doing something I'd regret for the rest of my life. He never knew the damage had already been done."

"What did you think when you heard Susie had been killed?" Adam asked.

George closed his eyes and tilted his head back. "I couldn't believe it. I had seen her alive and full of laughter just two months earlier. When I went to the wake and saw her in that coffin my heart broke. I couldn't understand why anyone would want to hurt such a sweet, giving woman."

"She was just a girl, George," Hick said. "Just seventeen."

"Did you think Abner Delaney did it?" Adam said.

George bit his lip. "Honestly? I didn't imagine who could've done it, but something about it didn't seem right."

"What do you mean, 'right'?"

"I just couldn't figure out what Abner would gain from killing her, or what would put it in his head. She could never have done anything to anger him. But then, I couldn't see anyone wanting to hurt Susie. I guess that's why I just accepted the fact that it must have been Abner because he didn't know her, didn't know the kind of person she was. In a way, I reasoned it made as much sense as anything else. But I guess deep down I never really believed Abner Delaney killed her."

"Did Susie often walk around Jenny Slough?" Hick asked.

"Never to my knowledge. I couldn't fathom why she would have been there in the first place."

"What about Ronnie Pringle?" Hick asked. "Could he have found out about you and Susie and become jealous?"

"Ronnie Pringle didn't care any more for Susie than she cared for him. It was their parents who arranged that little 'courtship'. Ronnie didn't mind sitting with Susie in that front room under ol' man Wheeler's watchful eye because when he was done there he could go raise hell in town. No, Ronnie was probably glad to be rid of Susie. But I don't think he had it in him to murder her."

"Did anyone else know about you and Susie?" Hick asked. "Did Gladys Kestrel know?"

"Gladys? Of course not. No one knew."

"Was there anyone else in Susie's life? Any one else ... she saw?"

George Shelley's face grew taut with anger. He turned hardened eyes on Hick. "Susie wasn't that kind. What we had was real. It was special. It wasn't tawdry." His nostrils flared and his lip twitched with rage. "You don't know what it is like to mourn in silence ... to lose someone you love and be unable to speak about it to anyone. I have lived with this for over fourteen years and have been unable to show anyone my pain. And now you tell me I lost a child?" He sunk down in his chair. "Must've been about four months ..." He covered his face with his hands. "My god." His voice cracked and his shoulders shook.

Hick looked at Adam and nodded toward the door. He crossed the room and placed a hand on George's shoulder. "I realize you were young and you made a terrible mistake. But it was wrong any way you look at it."

George turned reddened eyes up to Hick. "Please don't tell Liz. There's no point hurting her, too."

"There's no call to tell Mrs. Shelley or anyone else. The three of us in this room, Doc, and Rev. and Mrs. Wheeler are the only ones who know about the baby and Doc and the Wheelers have no idea you're involved." They left George sitting at his desk with his head in his hands. Walking back out into the sunlight, Adam asked, "You believe him?"

"Yeah," Hick replied.

"Me too," Adam agreed. "Which puts us back to square one."

16

Shafts of sunlight cresting the early morning horizon caused the dew on the grass to sparkle like diamonds. Hick sat on the edge of the porch, his knees drawn up, smoking his third cigarette of the morning. He had stayed in bed until the panic was unbearable. Unable to get comfortable, unable to breathe, his heart hammered so erratically he felt his chest would explode. Gasping for air, he'd tried to calm himself by imagining himself singing the nursery song Maggie sang to Jimmy, but his mind wouldn't concentrate and wouldn't calm. He couldn't form a coherent thought except that he'd been "Private First Class Andrew Jackson Blackburn, 37615944." All those things he'd done, the mistakes, the fear, they emerged from the darkness, just beyond the reach of reason. They danced at the periphery of his consciousness and taunted him, making rest, or peace, impossible. When he squeezed his eyes closed, the image of Job Delaney, a gaping hole in his back and dark, jelly-like blood everywhere, flitted across the back of his eyelids followed by the tiny bones sitting in a metal pan at Doc's house. Gladys caught in a tree, her mouth half gone. Finally, at four o'clock, he slipped out of bed and dressed.

He inhaled the cigarette deeply; the smoke filling the empty spaces in his lungs where the air had been pressed out. The cigarette gave him something to think about, something to do with his hands, and it regulated his breathing. He stared at it between his fingers and felt curiously disconnected.

Something brushed his arm and summoned his mind back to the present. "Hickory?" Maggie sat beside him, shivering in her sleeveless nightgown.

He tossed the cigarette into the yard and wrapped his arm around her. "What are you doing up?"

"I could ask you the same thing."

He shrugged. "I couldn't sleep and didn't want to wake you. I'm sorry."

"It's okay," she whispered. "It's almost time to get up anyway. It's pretty this time of day, ain't it?"

He nuzzled her hair and murmured. "Very pretty."

She leaned into him and he felt her warmth against his chest. He breathed in her smell, kissed her ear, and wrapped both arms around her, pulling her close. She was tangible, she was real, not a terrifying ghost that loomed in the night, but a flesh and blood woman whose very presence helped to chase away the shadows. Her lips brushed against his shoulder. "Come to bed, Hickory," she whispered.

"You said it was time to get up."

She rose and took his hand. "Come with me," she said in

a voice that helped Hick forget, at least for awhile, all that had happened.

∾

The morning light poured through the window of the station and across the stacks of letters from Susie, the year-books, and personnel and student records from the school. Hick was unclear what he was searching for because, in spite of the fact that George Shelley fathered a child with Susie Wheeler, it was not apparent that this had anything to do with the murder of Gladys Kestrel. In fact, the more they investigated the less clear everything became. He knew in his bones that Abner Delaney had been unfairly convicted which meant Susie Wheeler's killer had walked away. But did this have anything to do with Gladys?

They were not having much luck tracking the five thousand dollar check Gladys had recently deposited. The Central Bank of Memphis would not release the information before the subpoena was served, which seemed to be long in coming. The lack of progress was frustrating and it seemed their leads were vanishing. Gladys had been dead for almost a week and Hick feared they'd wasted too much time.

He picked up another letter and looked up as the station door opened and Wayne Murphy walked in.

Hick's lip twitched, but Murphy was not his usual cocky self. He crossed the room without saying a word and then stood in front of the desk and looked down. "Sorry to hear about the Delaney boy." Wayne lowered himself into the little arm chair beside the desk and studied the toe of his shoe.

"What do you want, Murphy?"

"I don't know … assurance, maybe. That I didn't have something to do with it."

Hick continued to stare at the letters in his hand and did not bother to look up. "Culpability is a funny thing, Wayne. Legally you bear no fault, so you got nothing to worry about. Go on and print your little paper and sell your stories … I can't stop you."

Wayne frowned. "You must think I'm a real heartless son of a bitch."

Hick didn't answer.

"I didn't mean for anybody to get hurt. Especially not a boy … a hungry kid."

"Funny how when you get people riled it's always the innocent ones who end up paying the price. The ones who seem to get in the way of all the madness."

"I didn't think—"

"That's right," Hick interrupted slamming the letter in his hand onto the desk. "You didn't think. You tried the Delaney brothers and convicted them in your paper with no evidence, no motive, nothing but a strong desire to make a little money. And the best way to make that money was to prey upon the fear and prejudice of folks. You made 'em feel like every shadow and every creak of the floor board was a Delaney comin' to kill 'em in their sleep. You whipped 'em into a frenzy and then you come in here askin' me for assurance?"

"I just—"

"Job Delaney was thirteen years old. He'd never gone to sleep one night when his stomach wasn't rumblin' with hunger. He never knew his father, his mother was an invalid, and his brothers were never around except at meal times when they would show up with the little they'd scrounged up to eat. He was easy pickins' for your fear mongerin' and hate. I got no assurances for you, Murphy. The outcome was just what you should have expected."

Wayne shifted uncomfortably in his chair. "I was just tryin' to keep everyone's interest. You know how short the time is before everyone stops carin' and then forgets."

"That's right," Hick said hoarsely. "They forget, you forget, but Jed and Eben, they won't forget. They've had a father locked up and executed and a brother killed. They'll never trust another soul and why should they? No one ever gave them a chance. Not you, not Wheeler … nobody. Yeah, your life will go on the same as always and tomorrow you'll be printing a story about someone's family reunion in West Memphis. But those boys' lives have been changed forever and they'll learn to hate everyone because of what people like you did to their family."

"That's not fair."

Hick sat back in his chair and crossed his arms. "Wayne Murphy you are about the last man on earth to talk about playing fair. I've watched you drive otherwise peaceful citizens to the brink of murder with your lies and manipulation. I've let you call me inept and incompetent over and over again and never said a word against you and you want to know why? Because life ain't fair and you're a fool if you think it is. I'd like to say I'm sorry if I hurt your feelin's, but I'm not."

"Okay, Blackburn, I read you. I didn't expect to come in here and leave your best buddy anyhow. And you still don't think them boys killed Gladys Kestrel?"

"The last time they were spotted they were pickin' strawberries, in plain sight, earning money to send home to their mama who they don't know is dead. Not typical criminal behavior to my way of thinking."

Wayne still appeared skeptical. "We'll see. I hope not pickin' them up right away isn't something you'll regret."

"I regret a lot of things, but givin' my fellow man the benefit of the doubt and showing a little kindness are things I'll never regret."

Wayne shrugged. "I learned years ago kindness is a luxury those of us in the news business can't afford." He rose from the chair and hesitated, then said, "Well, I'm off. Slow day for me. Maybe I'll have a stroke of virtue and write something nice about that Delaney boy."

"I won't hold my breath," Hick said, looking back down at the stacks of papers on his desk. He didn't look up as Murphy left the station.

Running his hand through his hair, Hick reached for a cigarette. Regret. The word echoed through his mind. Where had he heard it lately? He lit the cigarette and picked up the letters from Susie to Gladys looking through them again. *I know you're right and I would have regretted it.* This phrase had been lurking somewhere in the back of his mind, haunting him. After his conversation with Murphy the nagging thought returned. What would Susie have regretted? Was she going to expose George? Tell Elizabeth Shelley? Is this what Gladys was trying to keep Susie from doing? The cigarette burned between his fingers as he mulled this over. Something about it just didn't ring right. While it was true that Gladys worshiped the faculty and staff of the Cherokee Crossing High School and would have done anything to protect them, Hick didn't believe Gladys knew anything at all about George Shelley's involvement with Susie. Her strict sense of right and wrong would not have allowed her to keep the secret all these years and she certainly couldn't have worked for George with the same dogged loyalty. But what else might Susie regret?

Susie Wheeler could not have duped any other boy into believing he was the father of her baby and marrying her. It seemed George was the only man in her life. She was planning on running away to Memphis to have the baby and put it up for adoption. So where would regret have come in? What did she tell Gladys she was planning on doing? Whatever it was, Gladys was strictly against it.

A light went on somewhere in the back of Hick's mind and he caught his breath. The cigarette burned down to his finger and he dropped it onto the desk, quickly scooping it into the ashtray. He suddenly realized that Abner Delaney was not at the wrong place at the wrong time. He was there, in the woods by Jenny Slough, for a reason. "Holy Christ," he gasped as he jumped from his desk and grabbed his hat.

The open windows of the squad car provided little relief

from the heat as Hick drove through town. In the short amount of time it took to reach Dr. Prescott's home, Hick's back was drenched in sweat and the sun was directly overhead. "I recognize that look," Jake Prescott said as Hick climbed the steps to the porch. Jake was smoking a cigar on his porch swing and Hick sat beside him, lighting a cigarette.

"What look?"

"Oh, I don't know, that ponderin', pensive face you get when you're mulling something over. It was the one your daddy always pointed out to me. He would say, 'If that boy put as much time thinkin' over his homework as he did all of life's perplexities, he'd be a straight A student'." Jake blew a smoke ring and watched it float off into the distance. "He'd say it with so much pride. He knew you were destined for bigger things."

"Bigger things," Hick repeated. "Why do 'bigger things' always have to be so unpleasant?"

"Come inside." Jake stopped the swing and stood. "Let's have a drink."

Hick flicked the half-smoked cigarette onto the front lawn and followed Jake into the house. Dr. Prescott's home was his office and was impeccably clean for a bachelor's residence. This was due to Liddy Baker, the woman he hired that acted as nurse, secretary, receptionist, and housekeeper. Pushing through a set of saloon doors, the two men went through the kitchen and into the study, the only room of the house that Liddy Baker didn't touch. The ash tray on his desk was running over with cigar ashes and Jake squashed the fat cigar into the heap. There were papers strewn about and diplomas on the wall. The room appeared the same as the others in the house, the same paint color, architecture and much of the same type of furniture and yet it somehow reeked of masculinity. It was Jake Prescott's refuge from the daily grind of keeping the citizens of Cherokee Crossing in somewhat decent health.

Decanters of amber colored liquids covered the credenza behind his desk. Indicating them Jake asked, "What will you have? Bourbon? Scotch?"

Since Hick's last drinking adventure with Tobe Hill, he could not smell whiskey without his stomach turning. "How about Scotch," he ventured. "With a lot of soda."

Jake nodded and prepared the watered down drink before pouring himself a tall glass of straight bourbon. After taking a long swig he held up the glass and said, "God bless Tennessee." He and Hick sat in two worn leather arm chairs and Jake asked, "So tell me, son. What's on your mind?"

Hick took a drink and felt the liquid go down his throat. "Doc, are there any kind of tonics or potions a woman can drink to make her lose a baby?"

"Oh sure," Jake said sinking back into the chair. "Since the early days there have been ways for a woman to end a pregnancy. Most of them didn't really work. Just made her sick for a few days and then things progressed normally from there. On the other hand, some were lethal and still others were surprisingly effective. Why do you ask?"

"Do you think … what about Pearl Delaney? Would she have known any of these?"

"I wouldn't be surprised. Many are made with simple

ingredients. Teas made from marjoram or lavender. Parsley, thyme, all things she could have gotten fairly easily."

Hick took a drink and leaned forward. "Just suppose that Abner Delaney was in the woods the day Susie Wheeler died, not for some murderous reason and not by chance. Let's say he was there to deliver a tonic made by Pearl to Susie. A tonic to make her lose her baby … to make it all just go away. Isn't that more likely than just being at the wrong place at the wrong time?"

Jake drained his glass and rose to re-fill it. "It certainly seems plausible. Why do you think Susie would consider such a step?"

"Because in a letter she seems to indicate that she had at least thought about it. She tells Gladys she knows if she had followed through with some plan she would have regretted it. I can't think of anything she might have regretted more."

Jake sat back down and Hick went on. "The more I think of it, it just seems to make the most sense. When I told Pearl about her boys finding Gladys she said the words, 'God's judgment.' I didn't know what she was talking about at the time, but it could be she knew she'd done wrong in sending the tonic. It would also explain why Abner wouldn't file an appeal. He wouldn't want his pregnant wife convicted of distributing such a tonic. Considering whatever she whipped up was probably worthless, it's unlikely she would have even been charged. The sad truth is, Abner couldn't have known that."

"If that's true," Jake said, shaking his head, "then Abner Delaney died to protect his wife."

"And that's just what I think happened. But it still leaves the big questions unanswered. Who killed Susie Wheeler that day and what does any of this have to do with Gladys Kestrel?"

"Susie led such a sheltered life." Jake took a long drink of bourbon. "I wonder how she would have ever thought of Pearl Delaney. I reckon the boy, Ronnie Pringle, didn't want to marry her? He would have known about Pearl since he lived out on a farm near the slough. You think he put the idea into her head?"

"Ronnie Pringle never knew anything about that baby."

Jake lifted his eyebrows. "Oh?"

"That baby belonged to George Shelley."

"Ah." Jake looked at his glass meditatively. "Seems I remember your daddy worryin' about those two."

"If he was worried, shouldn't he have done something? Told someone?"

"Told them what?" Jake asked. "That he had a young teacher and a young woman that seemed to be attracted to each other. Your daddy worked in a school that was predominately female. I'm here to tell you there were times he found himself attracted to some of them. But to your daddy touching another woman would be tantamount to beating the one he had. He would have never done it, and I reckon he thought the same of George. Good ones always have a hard time believing bad of others."

"And Susie Wheeler went to the grave with all her secrets of infidelity and illegitimacy intact, and George moved on with his spotless record. It makes you wonder."

Jake sighed. "This town is the same as every other town on the map. It's filled with good and bad, but mostly ambiguities. Behind every door is a story that is never told unless there is immense tragedy, or joy. But folks mainly live quietly, without fanfare, lives that are never wholly one thing or the other." He pulled a new cigar from his shirt pocket and ran it lovingly beneath his nose before he lit it. He took a puff and sat back. "Every dot on the map is pretty much like another."

"And all the roads on the map seem to lead back to the Delaney brothers," Hick replied.

"How so?"

"Well, if their daddy died to keep their mama out of prison, it stands to reason the sons would be willing to do almost anything to protect her as well. If they thought Gladys had figured out what their daddy was doing out there in the woods they would want to keep the whole thing quiet. The shape their mama was in when they left … they knew she wouldn't have lasted a week in prison."

"Perhaps," Jake said, "but it's one thing to give your own life for someone like Abner did. It's quite another to take one. That's a rather large jump. They wouldn't have really known Gladys, and I'm not sure how they could have known what she was thinking. And it doesn't explain what happened to Susie Wheeler."

"All that's true," Hick admitted. "But the reason I've never considered them as suspects is I couldn't think of a reason on God's earth they would have to hurt Gladys. As far flung as it is, I now have a reason." He shook his head.

"As crazy as it seems, all this does give the Delaney boys a possible motive and that's the one thing they didn't have until now."

17

Hick hardly remembered the drive home from Doc Prescott's house. His mind was pre-occupied with the possible reason for Abner Delaney's silent defense and the senselessness of his death. If Pearl had manufactured a tonic for Susie, it was highly unlikely she would have faced prosecution for a concoction of herbs that may or may not have caused an abortion. The fact remained that Abner would not have known this and would have done whatever necessary to keep his pregnant wife out of prison. If Abner believed Pearl could face prosecution, then his boys would also believe it. The question was, if Pearl Delaney had broken the law, would her boys have known it and how far would they go to protect her? In a case with few leads, this idea had transformed the involvement of the Delaney brothers from material witnesses to persons of interest.

"Damn," Hick muttered to himself. "Why do all the clues keep leading back to those boys?" Slamming the car door in frustration, he climbed the steps and opened the door and was astounded to find Eben and Jed Delaney seated in his kitchen, eating beans and cornbread and Mourning Delaney sitting in a rocker holding his son. As he glanced around the room, cold terror crept slowly up his spine.

"Hey, boys." Hick forced his voice to stay steady. "Any of ya'll seen my wife?"

The kitchen seemed small and cramped with the amount of space occupied by the Delaneys. There had always been a kind of wildness about them that was markedly noticeable when they were indoors. They seemed too large for their environment and out of place like caught fish tossed into a bucket. Their hands were dirty, not because they hadn't washed, but because the dirt had sunk into their pores years ago, making them seem as if they were a part of the earth itself.

Eben Delaney didn't look up from the beans he was shoveling into his mouth, but between bites mumbled, "Yer wife went to Doc Prescott's." He glanced up from his plate. "Ya'll ain't got no phone."

Hick felt a little weak in the knees. "But I just came from Doc's and didn't see her."

Jed's hard eyes met Hick's. "I reckon you missed her."

A forced, strained laugh escaped Hick. "I wonder how that happened. Who's sick?"

"It's yer boy," Mourning said from the rocking chair across the room. She looked down into the face of Hick's son and said, "I reckon he's got the croup." As if on cue, the baby barked a harsh cough that filled the room. And then another. Rough tearing sounds that came from deep within Jimmy's chest.

Jed's hard eyes remained on Hick's face. "Iffen ma were still livin', she could fix that up right smart. But ma's dead now … so's Job."

The room began to spin and Hick felt himself growing sick. The baby coughed again, a sharp, hacking sound and Mourning rose wordlessly and went into the bathroom closing the door behind her. Hick heard the sound of water running and a nauseating wave of helpless confusion washed over him.

"Don't worry. She's good with that sort of thing," Eben said letting his fork drop onto the plate with a clank. "Just like ma used to be." He picked it back up and continued eating.

Hick lowered himself into a kitchen chair across from Eben and Jed. His mind reeled, like he was awake inside a nightmare. The setting was uncanny: he was in his own home with two potential murder suspects, his wife was missing, and his son was hacking behind a closed door. He fought to keep his voice under control. "How long ago did my wife leave?"

"Not long," Jed answered vaguely.

"Strange I didn't see her," he repeated, but there was no answer.

The sounds of forks clanking against plates filled the kitchen. "When'd ya'll get back in town?" Hick made himself ask.

"Today," Eben answered not looking up from his plate. "Went home, but the cabin's burned."

"What?" Burned?

"The cabin's gone," Eben repeated. "We come here to find out what happened. That's when yer wife told us about Ma ... and Job." He shook his head in sorrow, and wiped his eyes with the back of his filthy hand.

Jed Delaney licked his fork slowly. "Yer woman sure is pretty."

Hick's stomach tightened and he glanced at the door. "Funny she's not back."

Eben finished his beans and pushed the plate back, leaning back in his chair with his legs sprawled in front of him. "Good cook, too. We thank you for the meal."

"You're welcome," Hick said with forced calmness. "I'm really sorry you had to come home to so much heartache."

"It's a blow, that's sure," Eben agreed. "But Ma's been sick fer so long. Weren't much surprise in that."

"Job didn't do no wrong," Jed interjected.

"You're right," Hick said. "He didn't do anything wrong."

"And he's dead," Jed continued.

"Yes. He's dead."

"It ain't right," Jed said in a flat voice.

"No, it's not—"

"Job weren't bright," Eben told Hick, "Mourning in there got the brains between the two of 'em. But he was a good boy to his mama. He done his best."

"I wish they both would have stayed here and not—" Hick began.

"Job weren't the kind to live in town," Eben interrupted. "It weren't your fault. He just can't stand eyes on him all the time. Ya'll got any pie?"

"I don't know," Hick answered, surprised by the question. "I haven't been home …"

Eben straightened the fork by his plate as if he needed to do something to keep his hands busy. "Mourning says you and yer woman been a real help to us. Says you been standin' up for us. We thank you for that."

"Yer woman says you don't think we done no wrong," Jed added.

Hick looked at the two teenagers across from him. They were coarse and hard, they were dirty and rough, but as he studied them something inside confirmed what he'd believed all along. These two didn't kill Gladys Kestrel. "I don't," he said. "But half the town does."

"I reckon that's on account of Pa," Jed said. "He didn't do no wrong neither."

"I know," Hick said, surprising himself with the force of his conviction.

"Ma says no one never did believe it," Eben told Hick. "She told all them lawmen how Pa couldn't even kill the chickens when we had 'em. Pa was a peaceable man."

"We Delaneys got no luck at all." Jed shook his head as if accounting for all the sorrow in the world.

Hick well believed that statement. "What happened at the cabin?"

"Can't tell." Eben shrugged. "Maybe Mourning forgot to put out the coal oil lamp."

Hick put out the lamp himself when he and Jake removed Pearl Delaney's body. "Odd the house would burn like that," he wondered out loud.

"We Delaneys got no luck at all," Jed repeated.

"What will you do now?" Hick asked. "You're welcome to stay here. We don't have much, but ..."

"We thank you for that," Eben said, watching Hick closely, "but it's gonna be peach season up to Michigan, and we'll be headed that way."

"What about Mourning?"

"She can come along. Mourning's a right smart picker."

"She'd be a help with—" Hick began when the door opened and Maggie rushed in followed by Jake.

"Where's Jimmy?" she said, scanning the room.

Hick waved a hand toward the bathroom. "Mourning's got him in there."

Maggie's eyes widened. "In the bathroom? Why?"

Jake chuckled. "Because she's Pearl Delaney's daughter, that's why. She knows the steam will ease his breathing."

Hick noticed the change that occurred in the Delaneys when Maggie entered the room. Eben sat up straight and Jed wiped his mouth with his sleeve. It was clear they had been taught to respect women, and Hick was embarrassed by the thoughts that had been running through his head, and grateful he'd not betrayed them.

Jake put a hand on Jed's shoulder. "Glad to see you're well, boys. I am sorry about your ma."

Eben rose from the table and shook the doctor's hand. "Mourning says you took good care of Ma all the way up to the end. We thank you for that."

"Your mother was a very good woman."

"We'd like to see where you have her planted."

"I'll be glad to take you," Jake said. "Let me check on Jimmy and then we'll be off." He knocked on the bathroom door.

Hick's eyes followed Maggie as she and Jake disappeared into the bathroom. As the boys busied themselves removing the dirt from their fingernails with their pocket knives, he followed Maggie into the bathroom. Mourning was sitting on the toilet and Doc had a stethoscope to the baby's chest. Maggie was seated on the edge of the bathtub, leaning toward them, watching the doctor's face.

"Mag?" Hick called quietly from the doorway.

She rose to meet him. "Doc says …" but was interrupted by Hick grabbing her face. He kissed her forehead, her eyes, her nose, her cheeks and lastly her mouth. She struggled to get her breath as he smothered her with kisses. "Hickory?"

Mourning giggled. "You sure do love her."

Hick gazed deeply into Maggie's eyes. "Yes, I do." He pulled Maggie close, hugged her tight, unwilling to let her go.

"You're trembling," she whispered. "What's wrong?"

"Nothing. Nothing's wrong. You're here, you're safe." He kissed her again. Maggie searched his face as if trying to mine the source of this unexpected warmth.

"Well, it's not croup," Jake said as he finished his exam and Mourning handed the baby to Maggie. "Just a bad cold." He turned to the young girl. "You did right sending Maggie to get me. That cough sounds pretty bad. Appears you learned a lot from your mother."

Mourning blushed with pleasure.

Hick bent and looked into his son's face. It was flushed and his mouth was parted, but when Jimmy saw his father he wriggled in Maggie's arms and smiled a lop-sided smile. Hick kissed his forehead. "Get better, Champ," he told him. He rose and told Maggie, "I gotta go."

"I know," she answered. "The fire …"

Hick nodded and impulsively grabbed his wife and son in a bear hug, crushing the baby a little and making him cry out. "Sorry Champ," he told him and then asked, "You all right with all our guests?"

She nodded but told him, "I don't think the boys will stay here."

"Try to figure out a way to make them," Hick responded. "Feed 'em. I suggest pie."

18

A rich, oddly pleasant smell of burnt wood perfumed the air. Very little remained of the shack that Abner Delaney had built on the banks of the Little River eighteen years earlier. Heaps of white ash filled the air like choking snowflakes as Hick and Adam sifted through the rubble. Despite the sun, darkness closed in on the cabin from the dense trees that had grown up around it. The rusted pick-up truck was covered in ash, but seemed to have escaped the fire.

"You're sure you blew out the lamp?" Adam asked as they walked through the charred remains.

"I turned down the wick and blew it out," Hick replied with certainty. "I know because I remember Doc commenting on how dark it is out here."

Adam kicked at a pile of ash. "What else could have caused it? Was there a fire in the stove?"

"I put that out, too."

"You sure?"

"Positive."

Adam looked around him. "There's been a lot of storms recently. Reckon it was lightning?"

Hick shrugged. "No way to know. It's almost all gone."

The cinder blocks that held up the shaky foundation now stood like silent sentries along the footprint of the house. The floor had almost been completely consumed and the wood burning stove had crashed through and stood tilted with the oven door hanging open. Hick stood and looked toward the Little River. He imagined Abner patiently dragging up driftwood, log by log, and planing and hewing it into a shelter for his new wife. He thought of the optimism the couple must have had at the start of their life together, and the tragic way it all turned out.

Hick kicked at the rubble and felt an overwhelming sense of sadness. "Jed wasn't kidding when he said the Delaneys have no luck," he told Adam. Pausing a moment, he sniffed the air. "Do you smell that?"

Adam stopped. "What?"

Hick's stomach churned. Sweat beaded on his forehead and his palms grew moist. "Gasoline. Do you smell it?"

Adam sniffed. "I don't smell anything."

Hick's dinner washed up behind his throat and he swallowed hard and fought back the dizziness. He put his hand on his forehead and closed his eyes trying to force the earth to stop spinning.

Adam came beside him. "What's wrong?"

"Nothing," Hick answered quickly. "There's nothing wrong. Maybe I've got the flu."

Adam looked skeptical. "What all of a sudden?"

Hick shrugged. "I don't know, maybe. You're sure you don't smell gasoline?"

Adam again sniffed at the air. "No. I can't smell anything."

Hick closed his eyes against the brightness of the flames that roared up in his memory. He could hear them, like rushing wind, consuming everything … the old farmhouse in Belgium, the bodies within.

"What's wrong?"

"I said nothing!" Hick snapped. "Jesus Christ! Nothing is wrong. Just back off!"

Adam put his hands up and took a step backward. "Okay, okay. Whatever you say."

Hick breathed in deeply through his nose and exhaled loudly. "Sorry, Adam." He rubbed his hand over his eyes. "Sorry. Sometimes smells bring back things I'd just as soon forget."

"I know," Adam said, stepping forward and putting a large hand on Hick's shoulder.

The two men searched the floors, looking for any darkened marks, any traces of an accelerant, but found nothing. "I'm sure I'm just imagining it, or it's the truck," Hick finally decided. They sifted through the debris and Adam moved to the perimeter of the house, scouring the ground, looking for something that might be out of place, that didn't belong. He bent and picked something up. "What do you make of this?" he asked Hick.

Hick joined him and they looked at the object, Adam

turning it over in his fingers. Years of caked, sandy mud and a layer of white ash, obscured its purpose, but something glinted beneath the grime.

"I can't imagine the Delaneys ever owned much that was shiny," Hick said.

"Here. I've got an idea," Adam said. He went to the squad car and pulled out the Coke he'd been drinking. He poured it over the object and, after scrubbing it against his pants, it finally emerged from the slop.

"It's a cuff link." Adam held it out to Hick.

"Why in the hell would the Delaneys need a cuff link?"

"It ain't the Delaneys," Adam said slowly. He handed the piece of gold to Hick. On the front of the link a "P" was engraved in elegant script.

"Shit."

∾

The Pringle Farm had doubled in size since the Jenny Slough had been dammed up. The family had arrived in Cherokee Crossing before the Civil War and had remained in the same place, slowly buying up farm after farm from those who moved on or died. Even before the slough was dammed they had the largest farm in town and the Pringle men, tall, handsome, smart, were plenty capable of managing the land.

But wealth and prosperity had not shielded the family from heartache. Oliver Pringle had died soon after his son Ronnie and most said it was of a broken heart. Matt's first wife had died in childbirth, and his mother was now an invalid, living her remaining years in a bed set up in what used to be the dining room. In spite of all this, Matt retained an easy-going charm.

His young wife answered the door and smiled. Sissy Pringle was evidently ready to give birth at any moment. She was short and plump with soft, blonde hair and a bright, happy smile. "Good afternoon," she said politely. "Won't you come in?"

"Sissy, I told you to stay offen your feet. I'll answer—" Matt's laughing voice stopped abruptly when he saw Hick and Adam in the house.

He shook their hands, saying, "Sheriff, Deputy Kinion. Can I get ya'll some iced tea or coffee?"

"No, thanks," Hick said. "We were wondering if we might have a minute of your time."

Matt shrugged. "Sure. You want to sit?"

Hick glanced at Sissy. "How about we go outside?"

Matt's brows knitted but he followed the men. "What's this all about, fellas?"

Hick handed Matt the cuff link and asked, "You ever seen this before?"

Looking at it closely, Matt shook his head. "No. I can't say I have. Where'd it come from?"

"It was under the Delaneys porch. Their cabin burned and we found it. Looks like it's been there a while," Adam told him.

"The Delaneys?" Matt's brow creased in confusion.

"You don't have any idea how it might have got there?"

Matt looked at Hick and Adam. "I don't know how I would."

"It's like this," Hick said. "There's several families in Cherokee Crossing with last names that begin with P. There's the Presleys and the Ponders, the Powers, and the Princes. But, really, ya'll are the only ones who could have ever afforded gold cufflinks. They had to belong to your kin. I just can't figure out how the Delaneys might have got hold of 'em."

Matt took the cufflink back in his hand and studied it. He shook his head and said, "I honestly don't know." He thought a moment and added, "It could have been Ronnie's. He always liked to dress nice. Wouldn't surprise me if he had cufflinks like this at one time, I just don't know for sure."

"Do you know of any reason Ronnie might have been at the Delaney's?"

"No, but Ronnie was everywhere. He didn't like to sit at home. And he had friends everywhere."

"You've never seen the other one here, lying around the house?"

"I've never seen it," Matt replied. "You're welcome to look around if you like. I don't know what you might find, but I got no call in keepin' you out of there. I'll be as helpful as I can."

"We may take you up on that," Hick said. "It may or may not be important, but it's late and there ain't no point bothering Sissy and your mama with this now."

Adam and Hick turned to leave, but Matt stopped them. Glancing at the house, he said, "Sheriff, if you have a minute I'd like you to come with me. I want to unburden myself."

Hick flashed a surprised look toward Adam and the three men strode toward the large red barn that sat near an enormous soybean field. Matt opened the door of the barn and stopped at the entry way. He pointed to a beam.

"You see that?"

Hick nodded and Matt continued. "When I was ten years old, I came out to this barn and found my brother hanging from that beam."

Hick's blood ran cold and his heart seized up. "What?"

Matt stifled a sob, his eyes reddened, and he stood silent a moment. Finally, his nostrils flared and he cleared his throat.

"My daddy sent me to get a hoe. It was June and the garden was just sprouting. When Daddy said to get something you got it … fast. I ran to the barn and opened the door and there he was, dangling by his belt." Matt's eyes closed. "I can still see his face … the way it looked. It didn't look like Ronnie. It looked like some kind of monster."

"I thought Ronnie got kicked in the head," Adam said.

Matt's face contorted. "Oliver Pringle would never let the world know he had a son so weak as to take his own life."

"Why'd Ronnie do it?" Hick asked.

"Because there's only so much tyranny a man can take," Matt answered, his face tight, his voice bitter.

Matt closed the barn door and the three men walked into the sunshine. Hick lit a cigarette. Adam stuffed his hands in his pockets. Matt looked off into the distance.

Hick took a long drag, blew the smoke out of his nose, and said, "You want to tell us what happened? How it is this was never spoken of until now?"

Matt stood there, tall and handsome, with a beautiful wife and a successful farm and began to weep. "When I told Daddy what I saw in that barn he couldn't move. It was like he turned to stone. He just stared off in the distance and didn't say a word." He wiped his nose on his sleeve. "It was Mama. She was the one who said it was lucky Doc Prescott was in Memphis. She was always thinking. She acted like it was the best thing on earth that if Ronnie had to be dead it was wonderful that Doc wouldn't be here to see the truth, to see what Ronnie'd done."

"I can't say for sure that cufflink was Ronnie's, but I can tell you he liked to dress nice and be in town. He never wanted to be a farmer and Daddy wouldn't listen. They used to fight about it. But Susie was always there for Ronnie. She was a good friend to him, and I reckon the only person that ever cared to listen to what Ronnie wanted. I reckon it hurt him real bad when she died. I remember him cryin' after that funeral. And then there were the whispers that Ronnie done it. Between Susie's death, Daddy's pressure, and the town's gossip, I reckon it all got to be too much. And then Daddy died. People say Daddy died of a broken heart because he lost a son. That ain't true. He died because he lost control. Ronnie slipped away from him, and there wasn't a damned thing he could do about it."

Matt's eyes trailed toward the house. "Sissy's fixin' to have a little one any day. I don't reckon I care iffen it's a boy or a girl. It won't matter 'cause it'll be loved ... no matter what. I don't care if it wants to be a farmer or a ditch digger. I don't give a shit what happens to this farm when I'm dead and gone." Matt glanced at the barn. "Ronnie was a great brother. He protected me and watched over me. I think he'd want the truth to be told. I owe it to him." Matt turned reddened eyes to Hick. "I miss him to this day."

∾

Dusk descended over the flat expanse of the delta, the fading sun, red and boiling sinking beneath the horizon when Adam dropped Hick off at home. Maggie was taking the last of the diapers off the clothesline and Hick's heart swelled when he saw her. It had been a long day and the thought of the sadness that seemed to lurk behind every door overwhelmed him. He stood and watched her. She was thinner now and her hair was no longer fashionably curled, but the beauty and dignity was still there. She was faded and tired and lovely. Impulsively, he crept up behind her, caught her in a hug and kissed her.

"Welcome home, stranger."

"Jimmy feeling any better?" He picked up the laundry basket.

"Seems to be. But he keeps sucking his thumb. I reckon we'll have to break him of that."

"Just let him be." He put his arm around her waist and walked toward the house. "He'll be fine. Just let him be."

19

The moon cast bright patches of light on the quilt as Hick lay beside Maggie, unable to sleep. Adrenaline shot through his veins like lightning, his hands shook, and he tossed and turned causing the covers to get caught in his legs. He thrashed to get loose and Maggie mumbled. Sighing, Hick realized that sleep, again, would not come. He crept from bed and made his way to the kitchen, careful not to wake Mourning Delaney who was curled up on the sofa in the front room. He lit a candle and then a cigarette and noted, without surprise, that Eben and Jed had not returned. It was three o'clock and far too early to go the station. His eyes fell upon the Catholic preacher's folder which held the sad ending of Abner Delaney's life. Sitting at the kitchen table, Hick opened it. If sleep wouldn't find him, he would make use of the time.

He propped the picture of Abner Delaney on a coffee cup. "Abner, if there's something you want to tell me, now's the time," he whispered. The flame on the candle flickered wildly and made a chill creep down Hick's spine and he inwardly laughed at himself. Father Grant's large scrawl covered page after page. Much of it did not connect with Abner, per se, but to the general conditions of the prison. In spite of the carnage around him, the brutality, the torture, the rape, the inhumane working conditions, the separation from his family, and the isolation from any semblance of kindness, Abner Delaney retained his humanity. It was clear that Father Grant respected Abner, and his writing showed the frustration of being unable to help.

On one page Grant wrote, "I am certain that within this man lies no predilection for violence. He has endured humiliations from both guard and inmate and has not lifted a hand nor raised his voice."

Hick thought of Abner Delaney's baseless arrest and prosecution. Wash's words came back to him. He had said, Michaels was all about keepin' the peace and Hick was more interested in justice. Hick wondered if it was possible have one without the other.

"That's my pa, ain't it?" a voice said in Hick's ear causing him to jump and drop his cigarette. He quickly picked it up and turned to see Mourning Delaney beside him, her eyes fixed on the snapshot of Abner Delaney in his prison uniform.

"You ain't never seen him before?"

"No, Sheriff," Mourning answered. "Ma and Pa never owned a camera."

Hick looked at the photo. Mourning's only sight of her father was in prison garb.

"What you reading?"

"These here are notes that preacher who worked at the prison wrote about your pa. He thought pretty highly of him."

Mourning pulled a chair out and sat beside Hick. She picked up the photo and her thumb traced the outline of Abner's face. "What'd he say?"

"This note says, '*Today I, again, met with Abner Delaney. He regularly sends letters home to his wife who is expecting a child at any moment*.'" Here, Hick paused and told Mourning, "He's talking about you. Your pa worried over you before you were even born." He continued reading, "'*Abner is a perfect example of the injustice within our judicial system. Because of poverty he was falsely accused of a crime, and because of poverty he was unable to afford legal representation. In spite of this, he bears no malice toward anyone.*'" Hick put the paper down and turned toward Mourning. "That preacher believed your pa."

"My ma never stopped missing him," she said. "She hardly talked about him, though. I reckon it pained her too much."

"Sometimes things hurt so bad you can never bring yourself to talk about 'em," Hick said. "It's like if you talk about it, all that pain will come back and wash you away." He thought of Matt Pringle standing in the sunshine weeping. He thought of Tobe cracking open another beer. He thought of himself on his knees in this very kitchen, holding on to Mag for dear life. "Sometimes the best thing a body can do is to try and forget it ever happened."

Mourning put the photo back on the table. "That don't seem right. I reckon it will always hurt to think on my pa … and Mama and Job, but I don't want to forget them. It ain't wrong to be sad. It's just the way it is."

"That's true. But sometimes things hurt so bad you're afraid they'll tear you in two."

Mourning fixed her eyes on Hick. "But they won't." She stood and went back to the couch.

∾

The sound of the faucet running jerked Hick awake. Sunlight streamed in the window over the sink as Maggie filled the percolator with water. Hick's neck ached from sleeping slumped over the kitchen table and he felt disoriented.

"What time is it?" His voice was groggy, thick with sleep.

"Six-thirty," Maggie answered in a whisper. She put the coffee pot on the stove and lit the burner. Sitting across from him she asked, "Did you get any sleep at all?"

"A little." Hick rubbed the back of his neck.

Maggie smiled at him, reached out and touched his hand. "Did you notice?"

"Notice what?"

"Jimmy. He slept through the night."

Hick sat up straight. "Is he okay?"

Maggie laughed. "He's fine. Of course I checked to make sure he's still breathing. He's peaceful and snoring. His nose doesn't sound so stopped up today."

"You finally got a good night's rest."

"I had another boy up so I was a bit anxious. But I got a sight more than I'm used to getting and that's a fact."

Jimmy stirred and Maggie hurried to his crib and scooped him up. As Hick watched Maggie with the baby he understood Abner Delaney's predicament. Would he go to prison to keep Maggie out? To keep her safe? Of course. Without hesitation. To Hick, Maggie was a semblance of sanity in a crazy world. She had stood by him through all those dark days when he tried to push her away, through all the criticism and insinuations about his professional competence. She had been his childhood crush, his high school sweetheart, and the love of his life. He never told her what she meant to him. It was hard to put into words. But he trusted that somewhere inside she knew it.

"It's funny," he said as he rose from the table and pulled two coffee cups from the cupboard.

"What?"

"When I came home from the war the paper called me a hero. All us guys who came back, we were all heroes. They threw ticker-tape parades and told us we were special, but really all we done was live. We survived and that made us heroes." He glanced at Abner's picture. "I reckon all I saw over there and all I've seen since I came back has changed my notions of what a hero is."

"How?" Maggie asked looking up from Jimmy's face, her fingertips absently caressing the outline of the baby's chin.

"I reckon anyone who does their best, lives a good life, and doesn't hurt anyone is a hero." Hick poured two cups of coffee and sat one on the table in front of his wife. "You may be surprised to hear this Magdalene Benson, but you are a hero to me."

Her eyes widened. "Me?"

"You." He took a drink of his coffee and kissed the top of Maggie's head. "I need to get ready for work."

When he returned, Mourning was awake holding Jimmy while Maggie stood at the stove cooking breakfast. She explained to the young girl that the letters O-A-T-M-E-A-L spelled oatmeal. Stopping in the doorway, he thought of all the nights Maggie spent alone at the house because of his crazy work schedule and how companionable the scene before him looked.

"I'm off," he announced picking up his hat and pausing to kiss his wife good-bye.

"What about breakfast?" Maggie asked.

"I'll grab something at the diner." Stopping at the door, he told her, "Don't forget to keep the place locked." He stepped out onto the porch and paused. The humidity was already oppressive and the air stifling. The bright sunshine glinted off the windshield as he stopped in front of his car to light a cigarette. Even with the windows down, by the time he got to the station he was soaked with sweat.

∾

"Gonna be a hot one," Adam remarked as Hick walked inside and hung up his hat.

"It's already a hot one."

"We heard from the bank in Memphis," Adam said.

"The five thousand dollars was from a trust fund made out to Millicent Harris. It seems that Gladys Kestrel was an assumed name she chose because she never wanted the father of her son to find her. The baby's father opened the bank account in 1920 and put the ten thousand in it for Gladys—or Millicent, but it appears she wanted nothing to do with him. She never touched the money, not even during the depression, and I'm sure she could have used it. Apparently the man recently died. He was pretty well off from what I can gather. When she got the second deposit and learned the baby's father was dead, Gladys contacted the home in Memphis to try and find out where her son might be. My guess is she wanted him to have that money. Records are sealed up pretty tight. It don't look like her boy will ever get it."

"So what happens to it?"

Adam shrugged. "Gladys didn't leave a will and she has no heirs. I reckon the state will end up with it."

Hick sighed. "Damn. That was a pretty good lead … gone, like all the rest."

"You eat yet?"

"No," Hick answered. "Just coffee. Ain't got much of an appetite these days."

Adam grabbed his hat and turned to Wash who had been dozing at his desk. "Wash, you want to grab something to eat?"

The older man shook his head. "Nah, I'm good. The missus fixed me a huge breakfast today. I don't even reckon I got room for coffee."

Adam nodded and told Hick, "We can talk at breakfast and see if we're able to make any sense of all this."

The door clanged as the two men walked into the diner. The atmosphere had changed markedly. Rather than hostile stares, eyes turned downward in shame as the story of Job Delaney's killing had filled the paper and the ears of the town gossips. It was as if Cherokee Crossing had realized its collective shame in judging too quickly.

Shirley Daniels approached and took their order. After gulping some coffee, Adam asked, "So where are we?"

"We're in the yard chasing our tails like a couple of hound dogs," Hick said.

"I was afraid of that."

"Our suspects are dropping like flies. George Shelley, The Delaneys, Ronnie Pringle, and now the money trail has dried up. Hell, at this point I'm lost. What we need is a break."

"You hear anything about Wheeler and Job yet?"

"It'll be a few days," Hick said. "They'll make a show of it, like they're seriously considering the case, but Wheeler's got about a snowball's chance in Hell of being charged with anything."

"That's what I figured." Shirley returned with Adam's breakfast, and he attacked the fried eggs in front of him like a man without a care.

"Doesn't it ever get to you?" Hick said. His brother-in-law was not a passionate person, unless it pertained to his family and then Hick pitied anyone who ever thought of hurting one of them. He recognized within Adam Kinion a sleeping volcano that would erupt in rage if anything happened to someone he loved.

Adam took a drink of coffee and looked Hick in the eye. "Listen, Hick, if you let every injustice of the world eat at you, you will spend your life angry at everyone. There's all kinds of folks in this world. Good ones, bad ones, ignorant and wise, but we have to live and somehow get along with all of 'em. All I can do is work to see that right is done when I'm able. When I'm not, it's my job to understand what went wrong and do my damndest to see it don't happen again. We both know life ain't gonna be fair."

"Yeah." Hick lit a cigarette. "I thought that if Wheeler was punished for what he did to Job, it would make me happy, but it won't. Job's not coming back and Wheeler will live with that every single day of his life. There's really no joy in seeing anyone suffer, no matter how big a bastard they are."

"You know, it wouldn't hurt to go back to Wheeler's and go through Susie's room. We might find something."

"Good idea, Deputy Kinion. Finish up that feast and let's head over there. We might just find our break."

20

Mrs. Wheeler appeared haggard and tired, and yet there was a new-found strength in her face. "Have you come to take Ted?" she asked with an edge of steel in her voice. "He's in bed. He's not well."

"No, ma'am. We wanted to talk to you. Have you ever found anything odd or out of place in Susie's room? "

"What do you mean?"

"Any notes or papers? Did she have a diary, perhaps? We're looking for anything that might help us."

She stepped back from the doorway and let Hick and Adam into the house. Glancing upstairs, she said, "Sheriff, that room stays shut. I go in there once a year on the anniversary of the day …" Her eyes filled with tears. "You know, Ted and I couldn't have children. We'd tried and tried and went to doctors, but they all said the same thing. And then, one day, like a miracle, I was pregnant. When Susie was born it was like God had given us one of his special angels. She was always happy, always laughing. She was the light of our lives."

She wiped her eyes on her apron. "She fell in love with Ronnie Pringle when they were in the fourth grade. I always thought Ronnie looked at Susie more as a little sister than a steady girl, but they were best friends and that I know. They told each other everything. That's why I can't understand that Susie was pregnant ... I just can't. Ronnie would never do her like that and if Susie was in a bind, he would have done whatever it took to help her."

Hick's stomach tightened and a feeling of deep anger toward George Shelley filled him. George knew better and took advantage of Susie's innocence. He closed his eyes feeling the deep resentment boil within him and then took a deep breath, forcing himself to focus on the task at hand. "Ma'am, would you mind if we took a look in her room? There may be a clue or something in there that might help us out. Do you need to ask Reverend Wheeler?"

She smiled and shook her head. "Sheriff, take all the time you need."

The door creaked as it swung open. The air was hot and still, the windows were shut, but the closed curtains couldn't stop the sun's rays from illuminating the room. The twin bed was covered with a white, lace coverlet and a Bible sat on the nightstand beside a reading lamp. A Bakelite powder box, brush, comb, and mirror sat on the dresser beside a framed picture of Ronnie Pringle. Hick picked up the photo. Ronnie was wearing a bow tie and three-piece suit. In spite of the Depression, he looked well-dressed and well-fed. His hair was perfectly combed back and his smile was light-hearted, belying the turmoil inside. He had inscribed the words, "To My Susie, With Love, Ronnie," on the face of the photo. Matt Pringle's description of Ronnie's heartbreak and the photo in Hick's hand did not corroborate George Shelley's assertion that Ronnie would be "glad to be rid of her."

Hick opened the powder box and stared. "I think I found Ronnie's missing cuff link."

"Yeah? Well come see what I found," Adam said in a tight voice. Hick crossed the room to where Adam was seated on the bed. He held up a piece of paper that was in the pages of Susie's Bible.

"What is it?"

"It's an address … to a house in Pocahontas."

"You're kidding."

Adam slammed the Bible shut. "He knew. She was writing him. That son of a bitch knew all along."

"You don't know that, Adam." A phone rang downstairs and they heard Mrs. Wheeler pick it up.

"Who else would Susie Wheeler have known in Pocahontas? She was writing to George Shelley. That bastard lied to us."

"Now hold on—" Hick began when Mrs. Wheeler tapped on the door.

"Sheriff," she said coming into the room. "That was Deputy Metcalfe. He says you need to get over to Miss Audie's right away. She's got something to show you."

∾

Miss Audie was waiting for them on the front porch when they pulled up in front of the house. She was wearing the house dress she always seemed to wear and in her hand she held a paper which she waved the minute they stepped out of the car.

"It's right here," she told them. "Big as life. I never made this phone call. I can't for the life of me think of who might have made a phone call like this from my house."

Hick and Adam joined Miss Audie on the porch and she thrust the telephone bill at them. The Southwestern Telephone and Telegraph bill had the normal $2.00 charge for local service, but there was an additional trunk and toll service charge that was unusual. Turning it over to read the explanation Adam observed the date. "This was placed on May 30, the day before Gladys died." He knitted his brow. "Person to person. She wanted to speak to someone in particular."

"We need to call the operator," Hick said, "and see if they have a record or if anyone might remember."

Adam nodded and Miss Audie shook her head. "I didn't know that Gladys knew a soul outside of Cherokee Crossing. Who do you think she might have been calling?"

Hick and Adam exchanged a glance. Gladys had been contacting the bank in Memphis, the lawyer, and the children's home. But why would she call an office person to person?

"We'll look into it and let you know," Hick said. They climbed back into the car and Hick said, "Who do you think she was calling?"

"The first person that comes to mind is George Shelley,"

Adam said angrily putting the car into reverse. "That son of a bitch lied to us."

"Come on. We don't know that for sure. When we talked to him, we both thought he was telling the truth," Hick cautioned. "We don't know who she was calling or where the call went. She could have been callin' someone in Memphis where she came from. It could be her murder had nothing at all to do with George and this phone call may prove it."

Adam appeared doubtful. "George may have been telling us the truth, but still … a man who lies to his wife…."

"Agreed. We need to pay him another visit."

Adam gripped the steering wheel. "Today."

They went back to the office and Hick placed a phone call to the local operator in Pocahontas. She informed him that the call would have been routed through the Memphis switchboard.

"Who would do the billing?" Hick asked.

"That comes from Southwestern Bell in St. Louis."

"If someone were to place a person to person call, where would the record of the call be held?"

"The records would be held at the Memphis switchboard. The operator would have telephoned the rate operator and given the party the amount. The rate operator would have then switched the caller to Memphis where the call information would be copied and filed."

"Okay," Hick answered writing the information down. "Thanks."

He hung up the receiver and turned to Wash. "We're driving back up to Tennessee this afternoon. Can you call the switchboard in Memphis and see if they can track down who Gladys Kestrel called right before she died? It could take some time and I'm anxious to get on the road. We want to talk to George Shelley again."

Wash took Hick's notes and said, "You want me to call long distance out to the Shelley's if I hear something?"

Hick nodded. "Yeah. We need to get to the bottom of this."

21

It was dinnertime by the time they arrived in Tennessee, and they didn't expect to find George at the school so they went straight to his house. Situated on a quiet residential street, it was a white clapboard with an inviting front porch that held pots of marigolds and begonias. It looked peaceful and happy, the sun glowed on the windows with an inviting light, and Hick had a foreboding that he and Adam were bringing evil to that place.

They climbed the steps and hesitated, looked at one another as if they needed to reassure themselves that this was a task that needed doing, then Adam rapped on the door. The knock was followed by the sound of footsteps within and the door was opened by Elizabeth Shelley.

"Why Hickory Blackburn and Adam Kinion. What a surprise! Do come in." She stepped back and gestured for the men to enter the house. The front room was furnished with a sofa and loveseat covered in tight plastic. It was light and formal and didn't seem to be much in use. Glancing at the room, she told them, "Why don't you come to the family room. It's a bit more inviting."

The two men followed her to the back of the house, noticing that no one else seemed to be home. "Can I get you something to drink?" she asked.

"No thank you," Hick replied. "Is George home?"

"No," she said, gesturing for them to sit on the couch. She in turn sat in a stiff arm chair. "He and the girls are at the park watching the American Legion baseball team practice. After that they were going to get some hamburgers. I have a bit of a headache so I stayed home."

"Sorry to hear you're feelin' poorly," Adam said. He glanced at Hick and the look seemed to say, "We don't really want to interview George in front of his kids."

Hick nodded in silent agreement. "Ma'am, do you know what time they're likely to be home?"

Elizabeth glanced at the clock which read 5:00 p.m. "I don't think they'll be much later. The practice should have ended over a half hour ago."

"Would it be too much of an imposition if we waited here for them?" Hick asked.

"Of course not," Elizabeth replied. "Can I ask what you need to see George for?"

"Just some questions related to the closing of the school," Hick said.

"Really? I thought that was pretty much wrapped up."

"We just need to clear a few things up," Adam said in a reassuring voice.

"I see." Elizabeth's forehead wrinkled with thought.

"Seems a might eager you drivin' all the way out here at this time of day to ask questions about the high school. Is something wrong?"

"No," Adam answered. "We just need to see George."

"It's about Gladys, isn't it?"

"Partly," Hick admitted. "We're tryin' to figure a few things out."

"Are you … are you close to makin' an arrest?"

Hick and Adam exchanged a glance. "We might be."

"I see," she said and her eyes glanced toward the door. "And you suspect … George?"

"We didn't say that," Hick said quickly.

"But you're here."

"Yes. But don't make any assumptions … we're not."

"But I don't understand what George would have to do with Gladys Kestrel. They got on marvelously when she worked for him. She thought he walked on water."

"We just want to—" Hick began but was interrupted by the ringing of the telephone.

"Excuse me." Elizabeth rose and went to the hallway where the phone was installed. Returning, she said, "It's for you, Hickory. Deputy Metcalfe."

Hick thanked her and took the receiver from her hand. "What did you find?"

Hick turned as Adam came up behind him. He nodded, locked eyes with Adam, and said "Good work, Wash. Got it." Slowly he hung up the phone and turned back to Adam.

"Well? Did he find out?"

"Yeah. He found out."

22

Elizabeth Shelley rose when she saw Hick's face. "Are you okay, Hickory? Do you need a glass of water?"

"No, ma'am," he said. "Thank you, but I'm fine." The room was suddenly hot and his knees and his voice threatened to betray him. "Exactly why did Gladys Kestrel call you the day before she died?"

Elizabeth sank slowly back into her chair. "What?"

"Gladys called you person-to-person the day before she died. The phone call lasted for ten minutes. What did she say to you?"

Her face was frozen, a wasteland void of emotion. "You can't be serious."

"I am." Hick crossed the room and looked down on her. "But before we talk about Gladys, I have a few other questions. How much did you know about your husband and Susie Wheeler?"

The name Susie Wheeler startled her. Her eyes darted

from Adam to Hick and back to Adam. "The girl that was killed in Cherokee Crossing?"

"She was very close to your husband, wasn't she?" Hick said.

She bit her lower lip and waited, but Hick and Adam were silent. "How much do you know?" she finally asked, her voice hushed, breathless.

Hick knew he didn't have all the facts, but he had more than a hunch that if he told Mrs. Shelley what they knew she might break and fill in some missing pieces. He sat down on the ottoman in front of Mrs. Shelley and leaned forward. "I'll tell you what I know and you can correct me if I'm wrong. I know that Susie Wheeler was pregnant and that somehow she found out Pearl Delaney might be able to help her out of her predicament. I know that George was the father of Susie's illegitimate child, and I know that Gladys Kestrel somehow figured all this out when she was closing the school and going over old records. What I don't know is what she told you on the phone and why you felt you had to kill her."

Elizabeth's laugh was nervous and her voice shrill. "Kill her? Me?"

"You want us to talk to George." Adam's voice held a decided sharpness. "He's been up to his ears in this since day one."

"No!" Elizabeth blurted with a gasp. "Don't talk to George. He never knew anything about Susie's baby."

"But you did," Hick prompted.

Elizabeth's lips trembled. "Yes." She looked at her hands clasped in her lap and a single tear fell on them. She turned to Hick. "How did you find out?"

"There was a letter in my dad's study that named George and Susie as possibly having an inappropriate relationship."

She shook her head. "I had a feeling…. When Gladys called she said she thought there might be a letter that would help prove her allegations, but she couldn't locate it. I tried to go through there when I stayed with your mom but she was always in the house, always underfoot. I never had enough time." She closed her eyes and sighed. "I never had enough time."

Hick stared at Elizabeth. He had known her most of his life. She was a family friend, a mother, an intelligent woman. And she was a killer. But why?

Her eyes met his and she seemed to read his thoughts. "Did you ever wonder why George and I ended up in Cherokee Crossing? I met him in college—he was so good looking and funny. To me, it was a pleasure just to be by his side. We were married right after graduation, before we even had jobs. We moved in with my parents and started looking for work. He was going to be a high school principal and I was going to be a nurse in a big hospital. We had so much to look forward to."

Her gaze moved past Hick and she stared into space. "I didn't have stars in my eyes very long. I figured out pretty quick what I had married." Her voice cracked and she covered her eyes. "He had an affair with my sister … my little sister … in my parent's house. We hadn't even been married two months. We had to leave immediately and Cherokee Crossing was the first opportunity that came along."

Her face hardened. "He dragged me out to the middle of nowhere to hide his shame. There was nothing for me to do there. I didn't know anyone. I had no one to talk to. I wanted to work in Memphis. There was plenty of opportunity. But in Cherokee Crossing ..." She shook her head. "I hated him for what he'd done to me."

"Why didn't you just leave him?" Hick said.

She stared down at her wedding ring. "Because I ... I loved him. I thought we could work through what had happened, but it was difficult. We never spoke, we slept in separate rooms." She sighed and looked up at Hick. "But your parents were kind to us, and our church was kind. After three months we were slowly becoming part of the community." She shook her head and threw up her hands. "And then he moved us again. To Pocahontas. I knew something was wrong when George's 'great promotion' meant a huge decrease in salary. Money was tight and my suspicions grew. Then a letter came to the house addressed to him marked 'personal', and I knew. I read it. That's how I found out about Susie Wheeler. I couldn't believe he'd done it again."

Hick and Adam exchanged a quick glance as Elizabeth barked out a coarse, short laugh and shook her head.

"Who am I kidding?," she said. "I knew he'd done it again the moment he said we had to move. I knew that's why your daddy sent us away, but I didn't want to believe it, and I convinced myself I was imagining things. Until I read that letter from Susie. She was pregnant and distraught. She said she was going to see Pearl Delaney because the rumor was she might be able to help. Susie said she had stolen something of Ronnie's to pay for it … I didn't care what she'd stolen or how distraught she was. I knew once she took care of the problem everything would just go away. George and I would be together and it would be as if nothing ever happened."

She stood, smoothed out her skirt, and began to pace. "Everything was fine until the second letter. The one where she decided to have the baby. She said she had told the Delaneys she had changed her mind. The tonic had already been made so Susie paid them what she owed and said she was ready to go to Memphis. I couldn't risk her having that baby and naming George as the father. And I was terrified he might leave me. I couldn't have that, not with a baby of my own on the way. I just couldn't." She looked at Hick and Adam with wide eyes. "What would people think?"

She twirled the wedding ring on her finger as the story tumbled out. "George never knew anything. He only made problems, never bothered cleaning them up." She glanced up. "Don't think Susie was the only one. George is so charming. He even won Principal Knowles over. In two week's time, he became the model teacher, volunteering to sponsor every club imaginable. Of course, there was always some favorite or other—"

"And yet you stayed."

Elizabeth shot Hick a defiant glance. "Do you know how children of divorced parents are treated? I was pregnant when we moved to Pocahontas. I had my own baby to protect. Besides, there might have been plenty of other girls in his life, but I was the one he came home to every night." She waved her hand as if she could make it all go away. "If she would have just done what she set out to do, none of this would have happened."

Hick heard Adam draw in a long breath.

"As soon as I read that second letter I knew I had to stop her from having that baby. I drove to Cherokee from Pocahontas one afternoon when I knew she'd be walking home from school. I waited until she came down the steps. She ran over when she saw the car, thinking it was George. I offered her a ride and after running over smiling like that, she had to accept. In a way, I think she was just happy to be with anyone connected with him … even me. I could tell she'd have to leave Cherokee Crossing pretty quick—she was beginning to show. She asked how George liked his new school, and I told him he loved it. That he was involved with many of the after school clubs. Her face fell as I told her how glad George was to be away from Cherokee Crossing and how much he liked his new students. That there were a few who were particularly smart and he had started mentoring them. She wouldn't look at me then. Just stared out the window. It made me feel powerful. Happy."

Elizabeth licked her lips, and turned to Adam. "Do you mind if I have something to drink? My mouth is so dry."

He went to the kitchen to fix her a glass of water. The ice tinkled in the glass as he handed it to her and she took a drink and smiled. "Thank you." She peered down into the glass as if it held all the answers she was looking for. "We drove out of town and I don't think she even noticed she was so upset. I saw tears in her eyes, and I guess that's what did it. Those stupid tears."

Elizabeth took another drink and Hick noticed her hands were trembling. "And then what happened?" he asked.

"Those tears infuriated me. It wasn't her right to cry for George. It was my duty, my burden to cry for George." The glass slipped from her hand and crashed to the floor. Elizabeth covered her face with her hands. "I warned her to stop crying, I told her if she didn't she'd be sorry. She was frightened when she realized we were out of town. By then she could tell I knew all about her and George." Elizabeth got a faraway look in her eyes. "She was a pretty girl. I could understand George liking her. I put my hands around her throat and squeezed and squeezed until she blacked out. She never really even fought back. I'll never forget the sadness on her face." Elizabeth shrugged. "I drug her body out to the slough and found a rock big enough to make sure she'd never cry for George again. I made damn sure."

She looked up at Hick. "I didn't know until the next day that Abner had found her and told Sheriff Michaels. I was surprised when they arrested him—that was a shame. I wasn't counting on that." She reached out as if to put a reassuring hand on Hick's arm. "I didn't want Abner to die, I truly didn't. But what was I supposed to do? I knew he'd keep his mouth shut because Susie had been at his cabin. I knew he wouldn't want any suspicion thrown Pearl's way."

"So you kept your mouth shut and let Abner die in prison." Hick let the words hang in the air.

"Yes." She looked down at the broken glass. "Abner probably thought Ronnie Pringle did it, a lot of folks did. He knew Ronnie wasn't likely to be arrested." She puckered her bottom lip and added, "I really never wanted any harm to come to Abner."

"What about Gladys?" Adam said. "How did she fit in?"

"Oh, dear, good-hearted Gladys. She called me up to warn me that my husband could possibly be a murderer. She said she had a notion that he might have killed Susie Wheeler and that she was worried about me. I pretended to not believe her and she asked to see me. I proposed picking her up and we drove to the levee. She slipped out of the house right after breakfast for what she thought would be a short drive. I pretended to be amazed when she told me how she learned that George had taken a demotion to go to Pocahontas and it was right at the same time that Susie was confiding in her she was pregnant. Susie never told Gladys who the father was, but Gladys wasn't stupid. As she was going through those old records, she put two and two together pretty quick. Somehow she even figured out Abner's involvement. Yes, Gladys had all her facts straight, but one. The only thing she seemed to discount was that it might be me and not George that killed Susie. She learned her mistake."

"What did you hit her with, Mrs. Shelley?" Hick asked.

She nodded toward the fireplace mantel. On it sat a huge trophy with a marble base. The plaque on the base read: George Shelley, Principal of the Year. "George left it with Gladys because she asked for it. She wanted to keep it because she admired George. When she learned his little secret … she didn't want it around. She supplied me with what I needed to keep her from telling the world what she'd found out."

"But Gladys was your friend," Adam protested. "She called you to help you ... to protect you."

Elizabeth bit her lower lip. "I realize that. And I thought about it, but ... my girls. I couldn't let her expose George or me. I couldn't risk it. I never expected ..." Her voice faded.

"What did you expect?" Adam said.

"I tried to push her into the water but she snagged on that little tree. The ground was too soft to go in after her. I hoped she would just ... go away."

"This hoping things will just go away seems to be a pattern with you, Mrs. Shelley," Hick observed.

"Yes," she said looking down. "Yes, I suppose it is."

The sound of a car door slamming in front of the house was followed by the shrieking laughter of children and the happy chaos of feet running up the porch. Elizabeth Shelley's eyes filled with tears.

∾

The drive to Broken Creek, Arkansas was made in silence. Mourning Delaney, like most of her family, was not one for conversation. Hick stared ahead as he drove, speeding toward the shimmering ponds of humidity that he could never quite catch. He was tired, but Mourning had pleaded with him in her own way. What she lacked in articulation she made up for with the eloquence of expression in her eyes. Of course Maggie had taken the young girl's part in the discussion. A strong comradeship had sprung up between them in the ten days that Mourning had been at the house.

Hick was outnumbered and didn't even attempt an argument. He could rest when all of this was over.

The parking lot at Our Lady of Sorrows church was empty as Hick parked his car. Even early in the day, the heat and humidity were oppressive, much warmer than a normal June day. The day lilies were no longer blooming but there were now red geraniums planted in pots near the front door. Grabbing Abner Delaney's folder, Hick opened the door and he and Mourning walked inside. The young woman was back in the office behind her desk and her smile indicated that she recognized Hick.

Hick removed his hat and asked, "Pardon, Miss Esther, but is the preacher in?"

She rose and told him, "He's been in there ever since Mass, typin' away like every day lately. I'll tell him you're here."

She tapped on the office door and went inside. After a moment she came back out and and motioned to them. "He says for you to come in."

Hick entered and saw the priest, sitting across the room and typing with his back to the door. "I'll be with you in a minute," he said without turning.

Wordlessly, Mourning Delaney crossed the room and stood behind Father Grant's chair. Putting her arms around his neck, she pressed her cheek into the back of his head. He was startled and jumped in his chair, turning quickly. His questioning eyes met Hick's.

"This is Mourning, Abner Delaney's daughter."

She stepped away from the priest and put her arms

behind her back. Looking at the floor she said, "I never knowed my pa. Thank you for what you done."

"You were right. Abner Delaney was indeed innocent." Hick placed the accordion folder on the desk piled high with papers. "His boys are innocent, too. I found the killer."

Father Grant looked at Mourning and his eyes filled with tears. Sniffing, he said, "I've got a cold. Sorry." He reached into his pocket, pulled out a handkerchief, and blew his nose. He rose from the chair and put his hands on Mourning's shoulders kneeling down and looking into her face. "I'm sorry I couldn't have been more help to your father when he was living. And I'm so sorry you never got to meet him."

"You believed him." Mourning looked into the priest's eyes with her wise gaze. "It's enough."

23

Hick stood on the levee and squinted out at the wide expanse of the cotton field stretching toward the tree line. The sun sat fat and low on the horizon and the sky blushed pink and gold behind gray clouds that scurried south. The smell of warm, earthy, steam filled the air. The ground was still saturated by the last storm and Hick breathed everything in and held it. He exhaled slowly, lit a cigarette, and flipped the lighter closed. At the sound of an engine, he turned to see Jake Prescott's car jolting along the muddy road beside the levee.

Hick hurried down to meet him and helped the protesting older man to the top of the embankment. Together they looked down at the place where Gladys Kestrel had been found.

Jake stood for a moment and then lit a cigar saying, "What a damned shame."

Hick nodded. "She never was one to think much about herself."

"No."

"I wonder if her boy will ever know about her … ever know the kind of woman he had for a mother." Hick took a drag and watched the smoke evaporate, fading as if it had never existed.

"Adoption records are sealed," Jake said with a shrug. "He'll probably never know anything about Millicent Harris … or Gladys Kestrel."

"I can't imagine how devastated Gladys must have been when she figured out George fathered Susie's baby. Gladys was incapable of thinking bad about folks. And she died because she thought she needed to help Elizabeth Shelley. Always wanting to take care of everyone around her." He kicked at the wet grass with his shoe. "She was so worried that Elizabeth could be in danger because she believed George was a murderer. I wonder if she knew before she died that it was Elizabeth, not George, who killed Susie." He turned to Doc Prescott. "It must have broken Gladys's heart knowing that Susie was pregnant when she died and not being able to tell anyone."

"It's nothing short of heroic that she kept that information a secret all those years. That she was able to give Susie that dignity and spare the Wheelers that pain."

The end of Hick's cigarette glowed red against the deepening dusk. "She was a hero, and her son will never know."

"Most heroics are done behind the scenes, behind closed doors by unnamed folks," Jake said.

Hick threw his cigarette on the soggy grass. "I reckon." He stubbed it out with the toe of his shoe. "It's kind of funny … life moves on and it's the normal day-to-day drudge, and in one second everything's changed forever. One bad decision, one instance of bad luck, one overreaction and your life has changed and will never be the same." He put his hands in his pockets and stared out into the distance. "It seems like a completely different world today than when we found Gladys."

Jake stared at the end of his cigar. "Hard to believe we're at war again."

"I reckon if those men in Washington had to fight we wouldn't be."

"That's a fact." They were silent, both thinking of the latest wave of boys who would be sent overseas and the horrors they would face there. After a moment Jake turned to Hick. "I understand Maggie talked you into letting Mourning stay."

"Since Eben and Jed joined up to go to Korea and with another baby on the way, I reckon it's the best choice."

Jake nodded. "How's Maggie feeling?"

"Sick," Hick answered. "But so far none of the problems like before. We're keepin' our fingers crossed."

"It would have been better if she'd had more time, but I know how these things go. And Mourning … she's adjusting?"

"Maggie's teaching her to read." Hick chuckled. "Every night I come home from work, they're at it. I think it's good for Mag … it's good for her to have company. Mourning's not refined, but she's good with Jimmy and worships Maggie."

"How'd Mourning take the news about her daddy?"

"Better than me. Governor can't exonerate Abner Delaney because that'll get the state in all sorts of hot water on account of them executing the wrong man. Even in death, Abner Delaney can't get justice."

"I'm sorry," Jake said.

"Funny, but I don't reckon it matters so much to Mourning. That day she went to see that Catholic preacher, he told her the souls of the just are in the hands of God and she fixed on it. For years every person in town said the Delaneys were nothing but trash, but I find them to be forgiving where others would be vindictive and tolerant where others would be judgmental. I wish I could have done more … especially for Job. You know the Delaneys better than most … they may be poor and ignorant, but they're good people."

"It's hard to know from appearances who the good ones are and that's a fact." Jake bent and plucked a blade of grass.

Hick shook his head. "I think of all the shit that goes on behind closed doors … George Shelley and his womanizing, Elizabeth feeling like she had to cover up for him. I think about Ted Wheeler and the slap on the wrist the District Attorney gave him for killing Job, and I wonder what kind of world we live in."

"It's up to people like you to make it a better place."

A breeze whipped down upon them as they stood on the levee and Hick recalled Tobe's latest letter and how Chevrolet was putting on another shift. He knew he could get work, good work in the city. But there was a wind break of trees in the distance and the clouds above them mimicked their symmetry. The sky was enormous and golden beams struggled to break through the clouds to bring forth light that was as pure and bright as anything he'd ever seen. "It's beautiful" he murmured.

"It is. It's not perfect, but it's home."

"Home," Hick repeated as his thoughts traveled across the miles to a place he used to know. A place where his father's benevolence ruled and his mother made sure he was shielded from the darkness. The same house that now stood vacant with a "For Sale" sign in the yard. He thought of Pam's home, busting at the seams with a husband, six children, and their aged mother who could no longer care for herself. And his thoughts drifted to his own kitchen where in his mind he saw Maggie cooking dinner, her hand on her abdomen and a smile upon her lips. He saw Mourning Delaney sitting at the kitchen table struggling to read while Jimmy lay napping in the playpen.

He knew life would never be perfect. It would always be a sloppy concoction of right and wrong, anger and jealousy, misunderstanding and complacency and, yet, life was good in spite of it all.

The wind picked up bringing with it the smell of another storm and somewhere, far off in the distance, a long, low rumble rolled across the fields. Jake turned to head back to his car. "Best get off this levee," he told Hick. "It's fixin' to storm."

Hick hesitated a moment and looked at the place where Gladys had been found. Had the hatred in Elizabeth Shelley's eyes shocked her just before she died? Did it break her heart to find out that George Shelley, someone she loved and admired, had been a fraud? Did she wonder if she had been wrong about others, about Hick's dad? A fat drop of rain plopped on the ground beside him then another hit his arm. He saw Jake slip his way down the levee and jump in his car. He glanced once more at the scrawny tree. It waved in the breeze and for a moment he felt as if Gladys was with him. And then he turned and made his way down to his car. It had been another long day. It was time to go home.

Acknowledgments

Thanks to all those who have grown to know and love Hick Blackburn and asked for more. Thank you to my writer's group: Paula Birchler, Deborah Weltman, and Tom Boyd for all the encouragement, and to my readers: Bob Dilg, Angela Dobbs, and Steve Graham. Thanks to Ronni Graham, Katherine Ising, and Debbie Pilla for the support. Thank you to all who have given advice and help (you know who you are). And, lastly, thank you to Kristina Blank Makansi, Donna Essner, and Lisa Miller for believing in me. Without you, there would never have been a Cherokee Crossing, Arkansas.

CPSIA information can be obtained at www.ICGtesting.com
Printed in the USA
LVOW11s0134240316

480415LV00002B/2/P

About the Author

As a child, Cynthia A. Graham spent every weekend and vacation in the cotton belt of Missouri where she grew to love the mystery and beauty of the stark, delta plane. Today, Cynthia lives in St. Louis where she graduated Summa Cum Laude from the University of Missouri – St. Louis with a B.A. in English. She has won several awards for her short stories and has been published in both university and national literary publications. She is a member of the Historical Novel Society and the St. Louis Writer's Guild.

Behind Every Door is her second novel.